**The maid st** **bathroom,** **a** **bucket and**

He couldn't see her face, only the short cap of blond hair cropped close to her head. But the tailored lines of the hotel's blue uniform did nothing to disguise her slender figure, or her rounded belly as she turned to close the bathroom door.

The spike of adrenaline became a wave, slamming into Mason with devastating force.

Why did the maid remind him so much of Beatrice? Her hair was too short. And the society princess he'd met that night would never be seen dead working for a living.

"Beatrice?" he murmured, sure he had to be dreaming now.

The maid's head lifted. She dropped the bucket, splashing dirty water onto the carpet.

"Mason!" she whispered, looking almost as shocked as he felt.

It *was* her. How was that even possible?

But then all he could seem to focus on was her stomach. And his astonishment was overtaken by a visceral mix of anger and disbelief... And something that felt disturbingly like desire.

"Is that mine?" he ground out, on a rusty gasp of fury.

# A Diamond in the Rough

*Self-made billionaires claim their brides!*

To commemorate Harlequin's 75th Anniversary, we invite you to meet the world's most irresistible self-made billionaires!

These powerful men have fought tooth and nail for every success and know better than most how hard life can be. They've overcome significant obstacles, but will they be able to overcome the greatest obstacle of all...love?

Find out what happens in

*The Italian's Pregnant Enemy* by Maisey Yates

*Hidden Heir with His Housekeeper* by Heidi Rice

And watch this space, there are more seductive A Diamond in the Rough heroes coming your way soon!

# *Heidi Rice*

—

## HIDDEN HEIR WITH
## HIS HOUSEKEEPER

HARLEQUIN
PRESENTS

ISBN-13: 978-1-335-59231-6

Hidden Heir with His Housekeeper

Copyright © 2024 by Heidi Rice

Recycling programs for this product may not exist in your area.

For questions and comments about the quality of this book, please contact us at CustomerService@Harlequin.com.

Harlequin Enterprises ULC
22 Adelaide St. West, 41st Floor
Toronto, Ontario M5H 4E3, Canada
www.Harlequin.com

**Printed in U.S.A.**

*USA TODAY* bestselling author **Heidi Rice** lives in London, England. She is married with two teenage sons—which gives her rather too much of an insight into the male psyche—and also works as a film journalist. She adores her job, which involves getting swept up in a world of high emotions; sensual excitement; funny, feisty women; sexy, tortured men; and glamorous locations where laundry doesn't exist. Once she turns off her computer, she often does chores—usually involving laundry!

### Books by Heidi Rice

### Harlequin Presents

*Revealing Her Best Kept Secret*
*Stolen for His Desert Throne*
*Redeemed by My Forbidden Housekeeper*

#### Billion-Dollar Christmas Confessions

*Unwrapping His New York Innocent*

#### Hot Winter Escapes

*Undoing His Innocent Enemy*

#### Passionately Ever After...

*A Baby to Tame the Wolfe*

Visit the Author Profile page
at Harlequin.com for more titles.

To Rob, let's go back to the Italian Riviera soon!

# CHAPTER ONE

MASON FOXX STOOD at the eighty-foot-long champagne bar, carved out of a single piece of mahogany, and nursed a lukewarm glass of 1959 Dom Perignon. He gazed at the guests making pointless small talk and gorging themselves on the free cordon bleu canapés in the cavernous warehouse space below, decked out in fake greenery to launch a male fragrance which smelled like mould, in his humble opinion.

The former power station on the South Bank of the River Thames had been gutted and rehabbed a few years ago, and eventually converted into this stunning entertainment venue.

His lips quirked in wry amusement. Funny to think this ultra-modern, minimalist palace of steel and concrete was within spitting distance of the hole where he'd grown up.

He rubbed his thumb over the scar on his eyebrow—a habitual gesture which reminded him of his childhood, and how hard he'd fought to ensure he never ended up back in that hole again.

His smile became tinged with contempt.

Not one of these pampered narcissists knew what it was like to fight for every single thing you needed to survive. Then again, the hotel empire he had worked his backside off to create came with social commitments like this one, which were nowhere near as much of an adrenaline rush as living by your wits on the mean streets of Bermondsey. Truth was, he'd almost rather be getting a kicking at The Dog and Duck—where fortunes had changed hands faster than the packets of little pills with smiley faces on—than sipping overpriced bubbles, bored out of his skull.

Of course, The Dog and Duck had been bulldozed ten years ago, and Bermondsey was now as gentrified as the rest of Southwark, while the villains he'd been terrified of as a boy were all banged up or dead. But at least those criminals had personality, unlike the array of dull, talentless nepo babies, corporate suits and limelight hoggers who turned up at these events like clockwork.

He placed the fancy flute on the bar. Time to head back to the empty penthouse suite he kept at The Foxx Grand in Belgravia, or his equally soulless loft apartment at Foxx Suites overlooking Tower Bridge, if he was getting sentimental about the bad old days—and the villains who had once made his life a misery.

'Would you like a fresh glass, sir?' the eager-to-please young barman asked.

'No, thanks, mate, I'm driving. And don't call me sir,' he replied.

The kid blushed and let out a forced laugh. But then the barman's eyes widened as he caught sight of something over Mason's left shoulder.

'Wow,' the boy murmured, his expression awestruck. 'She's even more stunning in the flesh.'

Mason turned, expecting to be underwhelmed by whoever the kid was staring at.

He'd dated his fair share of stunning women, and in his experience looks were overrated—because they often came with zero personality. But then he spotted her too.

His mind blanked and his heartbeat slowed—then ramped up to about five thousand beats per second. Stunning didn't even begin to cover it.

In a fragile, floaty sky-blue gown which clung to her subtle curves and sparkled in the million and one fairy lights which lit the warehouse's exclusive balcony bar, the girl had the sort of regal beauty guys a lot classier than he was would once have written sonnets about.

He wondered if her skin could be as soft and luscious as it appeared.

The urge to plunge his fingers into the blonde curls perched on top of her head in an expertly constructed hairdo kicked him in the gut.

*What the hell?*

He shoved his fists into his trousers pockets. He might be more than happy to indulge his baser instincts, but even he had never wanted a woman with this much intensity at first sight. He didn't like it, because it reminded him of the feral kid he'd once been—always on the outside looking in at other people's perfect lives.

Her gaze coasted towards him, almost as if she could sense him watching her from the other side of the bar. And he got an eyeful of her delicate, perfectly symmetrical features.

*Damn.*

Her face was as striking as the rest of her. Her bone structure was like a work of art while the smoky gunk around her eyes made them look huge… And strangely guileless.

Which had to be an act. No woman who carried herself with such effortless sensuality would be unaware of the challenge her I'm-too-perfect-to-touch appearance would present to every heterosexual bloke in the place.

Her tongue flicked out to moisten her lips in a nervous gesture which would have been endearing if it weren't so hot.

It had the desired effect though, directing his voracious gaze to her mouth. Her plump, dewy lips glistened, and looked so kissable his throat became drier than the Gobi Desert.

He swallowed and sucked in a breath, annoyed to realise the rush of blood draining below his belt was making him lightheaded. But despite his disintegrating brain power, or maybe because of it, he could not stop staring.

But then those big doe eyes widened as her gaze finally connected with his, and she jolted.

What was that about? However goddess-like she appeared, surely she couldn't read his filthy mind from twenty paces? Before he could decide how to react—still spellbound by her artless beauty—she turned and disappeared.

For several heartbeats he stood like a dummy, staring at the place where she'd been, trying to figure out if she had been real—or a figment of his sex-starved imagination. He hadn't dated for over a month, after all. Not since Della had started making noises about moving in with him.

'Wow,' the barman whispered. 'Why do they call her the Ice Queen when she's so hot?'

'Who is she?' Mason demanded, wishing for once he took an interest in celebrity gossip.

'Th… That's Beatrice Medford,' the guy stuttered. 'Lord Henry Medford's daughter.'

Medford's daughter? Seriously? He knew Medford, in passing. He'd met the guy a couple of times at the exclusive Mayfair club Mason had joined a few years back, mostly just to piss off the posh nobs who hung out there. The man was a pompous ass who had inherited a fortune and then lost most of it… Because he wouldn't know a good investment if it sucker-punched him in the gut.

How could a woman that stunning have come from Medford's inbred gene pool?

'She's also Jack Wolfe's sister-in-law,' the barman supplied. 'They were engaged a few years ago, but he ended up marrying her older sister, Katherine, of Cariad Cakes. It was all over the tabloids,' the barman finished, falling over himself to answer Mason's question.

Mason stared some more at the empty spot across the bar.

*Wolfe.* He knew Jack Wolfe a lot better than Medford. They came from similar working class backgrounds. And, like Mason, Wolfe was smart and ambitious and a ruthless businessman. Or at least he had been, until he'd got married and had a kid, and softened right up.

He'd met Wolfe's wife too. And while the woman had an earthy, voluptuous, force of nature kind of beauty, which had obviously enslaved Wolfe, Mason would not have put Katherine Wolfe in the same gene pool as the goddess he'd just stripped naked with his thoughts either.

'Is that right?' he said to the barman, with an insouciance he didn't feel. Desire was still pumping through him in a way he hadn't felt in far too long. Maybe right back to when he'd been a teenager and had craved the kind of human contact he'd only ever found in sex.

The thought made him uneasy.

So, the goddess was a daughter of the aristocracy. If she were priceless antique porcelain, that would make him the knock-off kitchenware you could buy in bulk at any South London street market.

It figured. That had to be where the regal grace came from—wealth, privilege and a sense of superiority he had always found a pain in the arse.

Then again, it had been a long time since he'd enjoyed the thrill of the chase and maybe knocking a princess off her pedestal would salvage this evening's entertainment.

Strolling over to the balcony, he searched the

crowd. He spotted her instantly, her blonde hair like a beacon.

The warehouse lights dimmed and a world-famous DJ opened his set from a stage at the far end of the cavernous space.

Mason headed down the winding metal staircase leading to the dancefloor, already full of people moving to the beat. The music pulsed, while multi-coloured lasers slashed through plumes of artificial smoke, ramping up the throb of anticipation in his gut.

Of course, it was doubtful he'd still want Medford's untouchable daughter after having a conversation with her—given his low tolerance for snooty society princesses—but there was only one way to find out.

He spotted the blonde chignon taking the stairs opposite him. Was she heading for the exit? So soon?

*Not so fast, love…*

*Who was that guy? Looking at me as if he wanted to gobble me up in a few greedy bites…*

Beatrice Medford lifted the hem of her designer gown and shot up the stairs towards the first-floor balcony.

She really ought to be outraged. Bar Guy's gaze had roamed over her body with an insolent entitlement she'd never encountered before.

Men usually gazed at her with awe, or adoration. Because all they ever saw was the sheen of class, the shield of respectability, the sexless and untouchable grace which was all part of the façade her father had created.

But she hadn't been outraged at all—if she were being entirely honest with herself, what she'd actually been was…well, turned on.

Which was seriously weird for two reasons: she didn't get turned on by male attention. Because she got enough of it to know it had no real connection to who she was inside. And also because she had no desire to even be here, wearing this far too revealing dress and uncomfortable five-inch heels, simply because her father had demanded it of her.

She shouldn't have let him bully her into 'being seen' at tonight's event. Because she knew exactly what his decision to hire her a stylist and a designer gown at vast expense and demand she come to the Cascade Scent launch was really all about. It was just another of Henry Medford's increasingly desperate attempts to shore up his flagging finances by hooking his daughter up with the nearest eligible billionaire.

This afternoon, in his study, he'd even given her a shortlist of men he thought it would be suitable for her to 'engage with' tonight—his cold, assessing glare raking over her with a chilling mix of calculation and contempt. If that hadn't been enough of a wake-up call to his demeaning intentions, his preposterous list had included a three times divorced investment banker who was older than he was, and a boutique hotel magnate who'd dragged himself out of a notorious South London council estate and was well known for dating and dumping beautiful women with the same ruthless efficiency he'd acquired his property portfolio,

*Gee, thanks, Daddy, why not tell me you're pimping me out without telling me you're pimping me out?*

She sighed as she reached one of the venue's many secret bars and gazed at the throng of gyrating bodies blocking her route to the exit.

She should have told her father to take a hike this time. The way her sister Katie had been suggesting she do for years. Instead of allowing herself to be parcelled up like a mannequin in shoes that made her arches ache and a practically transparent dress and deposited at an event where she would rather fade into the high-end furnishings than 'engage with' one of the men her father had suggested, who were no doubt just like him.

As if one unconscionable overbearing bastard in her life wasn't enough!

She'd been terrified of her father once...

Back when she was twelve years old and she'd watched him rant and rave and kick her six-teen-year-old sister out of the house. It still disgusted Bea that she had done not one thing to help Katie, because she'd been too busy cowering in a corner with her hands over her ears, pretending to be invisible.

But she'd discovered in the past few years, ever since she'd asked Katie to dump the fiancé her father had lined up for her—because Bea had been completely overwhelmed by Jack Wolfe's forceful personality—and then watched her brilliant, beautiful and entirely independent sister make a life with Wolfe instead, it was past time she got a life of her own.

Which meant no longer kowtowing to her father's agenda—or relying on his money.

She wasn't terrified of him any more—and she had options now. She'd spent the last two years, on the afternoons she was supposed to be at the beauticians or the gym or 'lunching' with the 'friends' she had never really liked from her finishing school in Lausanne, attending classes which Katie had paid for. She had a natural ability for learning languages, her ear attuned to the nuances of pronunciation, her mind fascinated by the intricacies of grammar and verb constructions. And she hoped one day to make a career out of her skill. Although she hadn't quite figured out how yet.

Katie, of course, had also offered her a place to stay with her and Jack and their toddler son, Luca, at their home in Mayfair. But there was only so much of Katie's charity Bea could accept without destroying what was left of her pride.

Unfortunately, knowing she had no intention of attracting the nearest billionaire so he could shore up her father's ailing finances tonight was a lot easier than saying no to him...

She would find a way out from under her father's influence *eventually*, she told herself staunchly. But she had to do it under her own steam. Unfortunately, planning and thinking and then overthinking her options was one of Bea's super powers. Taking direct action, not so much.

She edged through the bar full of ravers getting into the groove on the throbbing retro disco beat.

Case in point: she'd totally convinced herself, while sitting in her father's leased car being driven to this event, that she would seduce the first unsuitable guy she met to show her father her love life was not his concern and manipulating it not a sound investment strategy. But as soon as Bar Guy had managed to kick-start a sex drive she didn't even know she had with one searing I-want-to-see-you-naked look, she'd totally lost her nerve.

*Fabulous. So much for Bea the man-killer! More like Bea the virgin prevaricator.*

No wonder her father thought her love life was still his to control, when she'd never had a proper boyfriend, except Jack Wolfe—and she hadn't even had the guts or the inclination to sleep with him before she'd got Katie to ditch him by proxy.

It would actually be mortifying she was still a virgin at twenty-two, still living at home and still relying on her father to support her—because learning five different languages without finding a way to make a living from them didn't count—if it weren't so pathetic.

She reached the other side of the bar and entered another long corridor.

Why had Bar Guy's searingly hot look had her flight instinct kicking in this time?

Because his attention had seemed different from other men she'd dated?

He was very handsome, in a rough, rugged sort of way, his tall, muscular frame perfectly displayed in the expertly tailored designer suit as he dominated the bar. But it was the dark knowledge in his gaze which had disturbed her the most—burning over every inch of exposed skin and making her pulse points pound in unison with her accelerating heartrate.

That hot look had been so exhilarating and its effect on her so surprising—because wow, she actually had a libido. But then his attention had become too exhilarating, and felt like far too...*much*.

She slowed her pace, still breathless but more than a little annoyed now with her latest display of total capitulation.

Bar Guy hadn't approached her. He hadn't really even acknowledged her. All he'd done was look.

*So why are you running away from him, exactly?*

Was this just another instance of her failure to stand her ground? And engage with life.

She gathered some deep breaths into her burning lungs to calm the sensations pulsing in her abdomen when a figure appeared at the end of the corridor.

Her heartbeat jumped, then shot to warp speed as he walked towards her.

*Him.*

Had he followed her?

'Hello there, Beatrice,' he murmured, the rumble of amusement almost as disturbing as the sensations now throbbing in time with the bass beat from below. 'What's the hurry?'

He stopped in front of her, close enough for her to detect the scent of laundry detergent and sandalwood over the aroma of sweat and stale liquor from the bar behind.

How tall was he? Because at five foot eight, she didn't usually have to look up to guys. But even in her skyscraper heels, he had a good few inches on her.

'How do you know my name? Do I know you?' she asked, then wanted to kick herself.

Why did she sound so pompous and defensive? Of course he knew her—most people did after her break-up with Jack two years ago. Because her former fiancé's whirlwind marriage to her sister a few months later had been forensically examined by every celebrity gossip column and blog from here to Timbuktu.

His sensual lips twisted into an ironic semblance of a smile.

'We haven't been formally introduced,' he said, although she'd already figured that out, because if she had met him, no way would she have forgotten him. 'But, according to the barman,' he added, 'you're the Medford Ice Queen.'

She winced. 'You have no idea how much I hate that name,' she shot back. Especially as, for once, it couldn't be further from the truth. She felt as if she were about to spontaneously combust.

He chuckled, a deep rusty sound which reverberated in her torso.

'Yeah, I'm not surprised,' he murmured. 'It doesn't suit you.'

Heat mottled her cheeks. But before she had a chance to respond to *that* comment, he added, 'Why did you run off like that?'

She frowned, mortified. How did he know their non-encounter in the bar opposite had spooked her? She might be a virgin, but she was usually an expert at faking the aloof sex goddess act... Just ask the celebrity hack who had crowned her the Medford Ice Queen.

'I don't know what you mean.' The lie would have been more convincing if she hadn't shivered involuntarily when she said it, and the industrial-strength blush hadn't spread up to her hairline.

One scarred eyebrow lifted. 'Sure you do,' he said. 'Did I freak you out?'

'I... I wasn't freaked out,' she scoffed, or tried to, not easy when her heart was now jammed between her thighs and busy doing the rumba.

The sarcastic smile only looked more assured.

She was so totally busted.

'I really don't know what you're talking about,' she soldiered on, attempting to climb out of the massive pit of embarrassment she'd dug for herself.

*Perhaps shut up now, Bea, you're protesting way too much.*

She pursed her lips.

'Then let me introduce myself,' he said smoothly. 'Mason Foxx.'

Foxx? Where had she heard that name before?

But then it registered. He was the rough diamond hotel magnate who had hit number one on her father's *Billionaires to Pimp Bea Out to Tonight* shortlist.

Shock was swiftly followed by another nuclear blush to lay over the first. Unfortunately, discovering his identity didn't dim the endorphin rush in the least.

She studied the hand he'd offered by way of introduction. His fingers were long and surprisingly elegant, despite the scars on his knuckles. The tattoo of a bird of prey in flight etched across the back was even more intriguing.

She cleared her throat and shook his hand, because it would be rude not to.

'Bea Medford,' she mumbled, the feel of his work-roughened palm making yet more intoxicating sensations streak up her arm.

'Bea, huh? That doesn't suit you either,' he said, with way too much familiarity.

But she was already getting the impression Mr Foxx didn't stand on ceremony much.

'Well, it's been a pleasure, Mr Foxx,' she said,

trying for dismissive—but not remotely pulling it off thanks to the streak now sprinting from her arm into her breasts.

She tugged her hand free.

'Has it really?' he asked, not buying her I-am-so-not-affected-by-your-nearness act. 'Because I got the impression you would rather injure yourself than make my acquaintance from the way you sprinted off in those ankle-breakers,' he said, glancing at her heels.

'Which begs the question why did you follow me?' she managed, the streak now heading straight for her panties.

'You admit it then,' he said. 'I *did* spook you in the bar.'

'I'm so not answering that question on the grounds it will totally incriminate me.'

He laughed, the twinkle in his dark eyes full of genuine amusement for the first time. It had a weird effect on the rumba in her panties, which rose to wrap around her ribs. Why did she get the impression he didn't laugh often, and very rarely without that sarcastic edge?

He dropped his head to one side, his all-seeing gaze searing her cheeks, but this time it didn't disturb her, it only excited her. Which disturbed her even more.

'Why did I freak you out?' he asked again,

the tone of his voice managing to be both coaxing and curious.

She shrugged and looked at her heels, trying to buy some time.

How on earth did she answer *that*? When she didn't know the answer herself.

She flexed her toes, aware of the pain in her feet.

On impulse, she eased her sore feet out of the shoes. Relief came first, followed by the sudden sense of freedom—and a single moment of devastating clarity.

She didn't have to be the Medford Ice Queen, or her father's puppet—any more than she had to wear the painful heels his stylist had chosen to 'engage' the interest of this man.

'That's better,' she sighed. 'High heels are the work of the Devil.'

The heady pulse in her abdomen accelerated when she looked up to discover she'd just increased his height advantage by another five inches.

'I'll take your word for it,' he said. 'I hardly ever wear them.'

She laughed, because the comment was so incongruous. From the little she knew about Mason Foxx, the last thing she would have expected him to be was remotely charming or self-deprecating.

But then he skimmed a knuckle under her chin to tip her face up.

A sizzle of awareness shot through her as his eyes narrowed.

'Why won't you answer my question?' he said, the mocking light dying—as if her answer mattered but he wasn't expecting to like it. 'Why did you run away from me?'

She stepped back, and he let his hand drop. But something about the tiny glimpse of vulnerability had her blurting out the truth. 'Because when you looked at me, I really liked it.'

Fire flashed in his eyes, then echoed in her sex. Alarmingly. Strictly speaking, his identity should have been a massive turn-off. But, judging from the streak now doing the macarena in her panties, that wasn't happening.

'And that's a problem, why, exactly?' he asked with the directness of a man who knew what he wanted and had no qualms about going after it.

His arrogance was intoxicating, though, because it spoke of a confidence she had always lacked. And suddenly she didn't want to be that gutless princess any more, who wore uncomfortable shoes because her father demanded it.

Or the Medford Ice Queen, scared of her own desires.

Or the woman who would rather second-guess herself a thousand times than step outside her comfort zone.

Or the girl who had been so averse to any form of confrontation for so long she'd ended up at this event, primed to attract this man for her father's benefit instead of her own.

Her father wasn't here.

He never had to know she'd met Foxx and had found him… Extremely hot. So why on earth did it matter whether Foxx was at the top of his hit-list?

Mason Foxx was the first man to ever make her feel this fizzy, sparky, delicious awareness. How could she ever make a life for herself, take command of her future, if she didn't even have the courage to own her own libido?

The way he clearly did.

'I guess it's not a problem,' she found herself saying. 'Per se.'

'*Per se?*' he said, that mocking eyebrow shooting back up his forehead. But the devilishly naughty light dancing in his dark eyes only tempted her more, to do something so daring, so shocking, so wicked, it might finally dynamite her out of her comfort zone for good—and turn her into a woman as bold and brave and cool as Katie.

*Go for it, Bea. After all, where has staying within your comfort zone ever got you but doing*

*your father's dirty work in really uncomfort-
able shoes?*

'What does the *per se* mean?' he teased.

'It means it's not a problem if you like me
too,' she managed.

Then cringed. Did that sound too forward?
Too desperate? Too needy? Perhaps she should
have taken lessons in flirting as well as languages, because she clearly had no clue how
to throw herself at a guy with any degree of
finesse.

But then the mocking light in his eyes died,
to be replaced by something a great deal more
volatile… And even more compelling.

Had she shocked this unshockable man? And
why did that feel so powerful?

He placed his hand on the wall above her
head, trapping her in the space. His gaze roamed
over her, and she had the vague thought she had
unleashed a force she had no idea how to handle.

But rather than scaring her, his thorough pe-
rusal felt exhilarating. Especially when she spotted the edge of another tattoo against the open
collar of his shirt—and saw his pulse throbbing
heavily in his neck. He was exhilarated too.

She gulped down the ball of heat forming
in her throat as he leant closer and whispered
against her earlobe.

'FYI, I want to kiss you senseless right now, Beatrice. And there's no *per se* about it.'

She choked out a raw laugh, the confidence she'd struggled to locate for so long firing through her system like a drug. She lifted her arms and clasped his broad shoulders. Then ran her fingernails across his nape, thrilled by his shudder of response.

'FYI,' she whispered back as she pulled his head down to hers. 'Why don't you, then?'

He chuckled. And she felt like a superhero, before his mouth found hers…

His tongue slid across her lips, caressing, insistent. She opened for him instinctively, her heart punching her ribs in sharp staccato beats as his tongue thrust deep, exploring, exploiting, devastating…

The adrenaline kick throbbed between her thighs and her breasts swelled. She arched her back, desperate to alleviate the vicious ache in her nipples.

His fingers thrust into her hair, to hold her steady for the delicious torment. She'd never been kissed before with such hunger, such purpose, such determination and demand. And it was staggering and scary and mind-blowing all at once. But as her tongue tangled with his and she kissed him back with equal fervour, the passion locked inside her for so long burst free. And every thought bar one went up in smoke.

*The Medford Ice Queen is toast at last.*

Mason dragged his mouth from Beatrice Medford's lips, his pulse pounding ten to the dozen and the desire flowing through his system threatening to affect his ability to walk.

He searched the woman's stunning face in the shadows, saw the dazed expression in the pale blue of her irises as her eyes opened. Triumph and adrenaline hurtled through his body.

She had been as blown away by that kiss as he had.

There was nothing he enjoyed more than the unexpected. And Beatrice Medford, the Ice Queen with the artless smile and the hottest lip action this side of the universe, was the unexpected on steroids.

He cradled her cheek, ran his thumb over her translucent skin.

*Yup, as soft and luscious at it looks.*

She jolted, her skin blazing, and he grinned.

Wow, she was so responsive it was actually kind of ridiculous—and strangely endearing. Even though those wide innocent eyes had to be an act—because no one was this transparent, especially not a society princess who kissed with so much passion.

'How about a drink?' he murmured, framing her face in his palms, unable to stop touching her skin, the texture so fine, so delicate. He gathered a ragged breath and captured a delicious vanilla scent which was sweet and sultry and addictive all at once. 'At the bar opposite,' he added.

The last thing he wanted was to take her where people could see them, but the pressing need to cool down before he exploded was at the forefront of his mind—and stripping her naked in a nightclub corridor was probably out.

But if she didn't stop staring at him with the sheen of passion dilating her pupils to black, he was not going to be able to walk very far.

She licked her lips, making the pain pulse in his groin.

'Could we…? Could we go somewhere private?' she said.

His mind blanked for a second. And the pain surged.

It was the last thing he'd expected her to say. But then she'd been much more forthright than he'd anticipated already.

'How about my place?' he said, before he could second-guess himself.

She had to know going somewhere private was going to create temptations they would have a hard time resisting. But even he didn't usually move this fast. That said, it had been a long time since he'd been blown away by a simple kiss.

'FYI, though, that could be dangerous,' he added, to make it absolutely clear where this was headed if they ended up anywhere alone.

She blinked, her eyes still dazed with passion and something that looked weirdly like determination.

'Dangerous is what I want,' she said, the husky whisper promising so much heaven, he was sure he'd go straight to hell if he didn't take her up on it.

'Understood,' he said, and scooped her into his arms.

She yelped. 'Mr Foxx, what are you doing?' she said, forced to throw her arm around his shoulders.

'*Mr?* Seriously, Princess? Don't you think we've gone beyond that?' he asked, enjoying her indignation—a lot.

He marched down the corridor towards the exit, with her squirming deliciously, the backless gown sending a whole new level of torture through his system.

'*Mason,*' she said, sending him a stern look, which did not slow his heartrate one bit. 'You don't have to carry me…'

'Sure I do. It's quicker, it's safer—because you're barefoot—' he said, pleased he could make a reasoned argument when his brain was starting to disintegrate. 'And I like the feel of you in my arms.'

'Really?' she said, with that odd combination of awareness and surprise. Why was that so captivating? When it couldn't be genuine.

'Yeah, really.' He glanced down as he bumped open the door to the emergency staircase with his backside and caught her staring—avidly— at the barbed wire tattooed on his collarbone, which he'd once thought was cool.

He had come to hate the low-rent design, had considered having it removed for years, but as he saw the fascination in her eyes, he knocked it right off his to-do list.

'Stop wriggling,' he added. 'I wouldn't want to drop you on your very nice backside.'

She huffed, but tightened the arm looped around his shoulders as he jogged down the stairs.

When they reached the ground floor, he was forced to carry her back into the fury of the dancefloor. The DJ was pumping out a club classic. But as he toted her through the crowd, he became aware of camera phones lighting up as people noticed them.

'You can put me down now,' he heard her shout, but allowed the words to get swallowed by the music.

He didn't want to put her down. Didn't want to risk losing the adrenaline rush of anticipation which was making him ache.

At last, he stepped onto the building's forecourt and the night air hit—helping to cool the increasingly problematic heat. His shiny new SUV appeared, and the valet leapt out to whisk open the passenger door.

He was forced to relinquish her, and deposit her in the front seat.

'Buckle up, Beatrice,' he said, not even winded despite the fact he'd just carried her the length of the building. He pulled his wallet from his jacket and handed the valet a fifty-pound tip. 'Cheers, mate.'

'Thank you, Mr Foxx. Have a great evening,' the teenager said.

*Oh, I intend to*, he thought, the anticipation starting to choke him.

He skirted the bonnet and climbed into the driver's seat. Then turned to his guest. The spurt of pride and possessiveness shocked him a little as he took stock of her, looking serene and elegant and yet so perfect sitting in his car.

But as he closed the door and started the ignition, he forced himself to get the foolish spurt of pride under control.

*Just a one-night booty call, Mase.*

And not a foregone conclusion at that, because this woman had more class than he could even dream of.

He shifted into gear and roared away from the kerb.

The lights of old warehouses which had been turned into luxury flats flickered over the car's new paintwork as they drove along the river. These same warehouses had been derelict when he was a boy, the broken glass and rubble becoming his own personal adventure playground. Their newly pointed facades and gleaming glasswork reminded him he was no longer that feral kid, but a rich man in control of his own destiny.

So what if he wanted Beatrice Medford...*a lot*? Didn't mean he needed her. At all.

# CHAPTER TWO

MASON SLOTTED THE SUV into one of his reserved spaces in Foxx Suites' underground car park. Anticipation and arousal charged through his veins as he turned to his passenger—which was daft, the woman had agreed to a nightcap, nothing more.

She hadn't spoken during the ten-minute drive from Bermondsey. Perhaps she was regretting what he had guessed was a rash decision the minute she'd made it.

He'd seen the spark of rebellion in her eyes, and had found it almost as captivating as the flush still heating those high cheekbones. Her bright blue eyes were sheened with an intoxicating combination of determination… And innocence.

What *was* that about? Surely it had to be a trick of the light? Or the clever glitter of make-up which made her eyes look so huge?

Because she couldn't be innocent. She was

in her twenties by his reckoning, and had been engaged to Jack Wolfe once upon a time. And if there was one thing he knew about Wolfe, the guy wasn't the type to offer marriage without making sure he was compatible with his fiancée in bed.

'If you've changed your mind, I'll take you home,' he said abruptly, irritated by the wave of disappointment… And the spurt of jealousy at the thought she had once belonged to Wolfe.

Why should he care? He wasn't the possessive type.

And he preferred his women to have experience, to know what they wanted, so he could give it to them. Assuming, of course, he was going to get lucky tonight, which did not look likely any more, when her teeth dug into her bottom lip.

Heat surged into his groin, which annoyed him more.

He shifted in his seat, perplexed to realise her indecision was actually turning him on more, not less.

'I don't want to go home,' she said.

He nodded. And the need did a victory lap in his groin.

Climbing out of the car, he took a moment to get a hold of himself. He wasn't an untried kid. Not any more. And he didn't lose his cool with women, no matter how captivating or classy they were.

She probably just saw him as a bit of rough. A guy who was much more basic and straightforward than the posh boys she usually dated.

Of course, the fact she'd been engaged to Wolfe meant this wouldn't be the first time she'd lowered her social standards.

He frowned as he rounded the front of the car.

*Stop getting hung up on Wolfe. And the fact she's a lot posher than you are.*

Since when had he ever cared about all that class crap?

He reached the passenger door, intending to open it for her—he could mind his manners if he felt like it—when it swung open and her bare foot appeared.

'Hey.' He stepped in front of her before her feet could land on the cold, filthy concrete. 'Not so fast, Princess.'

Her bright blue gaze snapped to his face. 'I'm not a princess. I'm merely the daughter of a lord. And not even a very impressive one'

He chuckled. He couldn't help it. How could she look even more stunning when she was telling him off?

'Duly noted,' he said, then lifted her off the seat before she could object.

'Mason, what are you doing?' she demanded as he strode towards the lift.

'Getting you from A to B,' he said, grinning down at her perturbed face as he inhaled another lungful of the glorious scent he'd noticed in the club. It reminded him of the cupcake stall under the railway arches near where he'd grown up. He'd loved going there every Sunday, to help out Mrs Archer, the nice lady who owned it, so he could earn a few bob and stuff himself with the leftovers she hadn't sold at the end of the day.

'Just for the record... I don't need you to carry me everywhere,' she said. Awareness surged through him again at her perplexed expression.

'Yeah, I know,' he said. 'But I like carrying you, remember,' he finished, surprised to realise it wasn't a joke.

He'd enjoyed having her cradled in his arms as they'd made their way across the dancefloor. And not just because she'd been all soft and fragrant and wriggly—but because he'd liked the attention from the crowd. For once, he hadn't minded people taking photos, because they had assumed Beatrice Medford was his...

'Well, thanks,' she huffed, not impressed with his compliment.

It was his turn to frown, though, as the lift doors opened and he stepped inside with her.

*Why had he wanted complete strangers to assume he was dating Beatrice Medford?*

He didn't need to impress anyone with the women he dated. And she wasn't even his. Not yet anyway.

He put her down, and her bare feet landed on the lift's luxury carpeting.

'Plus, I wouldn't want you getting your feet dirty,' he added, to cover the gaff.

'My feet really aren't that delicate,' she said. 'But thank you, I appreciate your chivalry,' she added, looking more disturbed than thankful.

*Chivalry? Yeah, right.*

The compliment was so inaccurate, he didn't know whether to be amused or appalled. He pressed his key card to the reader to access the penthouse—and give himself a moment to calm down.

Something about her polite thank you, though, had irritated him too.

Had he read her wrong? Had the spark of anticipation in her expression when she'd suggested going to his place all been in his head, thanks to an inferiority complex he hadn't even realised he had until about five seconds ago?

He stabbed the penthouse button. The lift whisked upwards.

She dragged in an audible breath as the glass box surged out of the basement complex and climbed the outside of the old wharf building which Foxx Group had remodelled five years ago. The scenic lift gave them an enviable view of the London skyline at night.

Across the river, the Tower of London's majestic turrets were spotlit in the red and blue of the Union flag. It looked stoic and forbidding, its walled garden dwarfed by the sprawling office complexes that surrounded it. In the foreground, the centuries-old architectural splendour of Tower Bridge winched upward to let a boat pass through the Pool of London and continue its journey up-river.

'Wow! That's…amazing,' she murmured.

He'd grown used to the spectacular view over the last couple of years but, as her face brightened, pride and achievement swelled in his chest.

This was *his* city, its history and elegance now as much a part of his life as its squalor and violence had been nearly twenty years ago. And this part of it—this breathtaking view—was something he'd worked to earn, right from the day he'd got his first proper job using a fake ID, aged fourteen, to work as a bellboy in the Jones Tower Hotel next door, named after the bridge's designer Horace Jones. And renamed the Foxx-Jones five years ago, when it became his.

'Yeah, not bad,' he said with deliberate insouciance.

She glanced over her shoulder and sent him a grin which had his heart bobbing.

She was even more stunning when she smiled.

The lift glided to a stop, but he couldn't seem to detach his gaze from hers.

Her skin glowed in the half-light and he could see her pulse pounding in the delicate well of her collarbone. Her blonde updo had come undone during their exit from the club, the escaped tendrils clinging to her neck and accentuating its swanlike grace. His gaze dropped to the glimpse of cleavage above the provocative neckline of the gossamer gown.

What would she taste like if he kissed her there? At the base of her throat where her pulse fluttered. Would she be rich and sweet, like Mrs Archer's cupcakes on a hot summer day, or fresh and exotic, like the icy pineapple juice she'd given him to wash them down with?

Awareness flared in the pure cerulean blue of her eyes, along with the spark of determination and anticipation. And suddenly he knew. She wanted him with the same intensity.

The lift doors opened, but did nothing to break the spell.

He directed her into the lavish open-plan

space he had helped design himself. The sparsely furnished room was dominated by a glass wall leading to a terrace which ran the length of the building and made the most of the view across the Thames.

'After you, Princess,' he murmured, but the mocking name came out on a husky breath.

Because what he saw as she stepped into his home, still clutching her shoes, the dress clinging to her in all the right places, wasn't an Ice Queen but a flesh and blood woman, eager to explore their chemistry.

He took off his jacket and dumped it on one of the leather sofas, the tailored fabric suddenly feeling like a straitjacket. Undoing the cuffs of his shirt, he rolled up the sleeves and crossed to the bar, more than ready now to explore that livewire connection too.

'So, what's your poison, Princess?' Mason Foxx asked in that low voice which seemed to hold a thousand and one promises Bea couldn't quite fathom. But also didn't want to ignore.

Was he toying with her? Perhaps she ought to be more cautious? After all, she'd never been alone with a man like him, a man so forceful and rugged and assured he made no bones about what he wanted. Plus, all she really knew about him was that her father had asked her to seduce him, and his kiss had the power to make her forget everything but the feel of his lips on hers.

But despite all the potent sexual energy which emanated from him, she sensed Mason Foxx had a core of pride which made her positive he wouldn't take advantage of her.

Even though she had already asked him to.

She'd been in his arms twice already. And, despite her protests, she'd loved the surge of adrenaline, the shudder of awareness, as he'd carried her with that audacious sense of entitlement.

Surely the kinetic energy which made her body feel alive and languid at one and the same time was what Katie had told her about? The 'sex is incredible when you do it right, sis' thing Bea had convinced herself she would never experience.

Odd to think she should feel it for this man. Why would her libido finally awaken for Mason Foxx? Perhaps because he was so overpowering. Hot enough to thaw out an Ice Queen— even one who had begun to believe she might be asexual.

One thing was certain. It didn't matter any more that he was one of the men on her father's list. Because she had no intention of telling her father about tonight. Sleeping with Mason Foxx to satisfy her own desires—rather than her father's investment opportunities—suddenly felt like the ultimate act of rebellion. The perfect way to stake a claim to her own sex life for once. Or at least it had in the club, when she'd asked him to bring her here…

'A glass of wine would be great,' she said, licking her lips nervously, aware of his gaze straying to her mouth.

'White or red?'

'Um…' The question threw her, because she rarely drank. 'White, I guess,' she said, deciding something chilled would probably be a good idea, given that her body felt as if it were on fire.

He nodded, then opened a fridge beneath the bar which held an array of expensive-looking bottles. He selected one, uncorked it—using one of those minimalist corkscrews she'd only ever seen waiters use—then poured the golden liquid into a long-stemmed glass.

He handed it to her, then poured himself a glass too. She took a sip. The fresh buttery flavours burst on her tongue.

'What do you think?' he asked.

'Delicious.'

'Good.' He swirled the wine in his own glass, took a taste, then smiled as she took another gulp, mostly to keep her hands busy. 'It's a Montrachet Grand Cru,' he said. 'It ought to taste good—it goes for over a grand a bottle at the bar in the Foxx-Jones Hotel next door.'

'It...*what*?' she sputtered, then coughed. 'You're joking?' she wheezed as he patted her back.

'Nope,' he said, smiling.

'Oh, God, I think I just choked on at least a hundred pounds' worth,' she said.

He laughed, that rich, throaty, rare laugh which made her heart bounce.

'Not a problem,' he said. 'I've got a whole case of it.'

'That's not even funny,' she said, although she couldn't help smiling back at him.

'So, you and Jack Wolfe—what was *that* about?' he asked, the change of subject so abrupt she almost got whiplash. 'Because I can't see you shackled for life to a reprobate like him,' he added in an easy, jokey tone which did nothing to disguise the sharp look in his eyes.

Which were dark green, not brown, as she had originally assumed.

'Jack's not a reprobate,' she said, struggling not to drown in the vivid emerald hue of his irises, which reminded her of the chalk hills near Medford Manor in Wiltshire in spring.

'So, you've still got feelings for him?' he commented, the tone still conversational, but the sharp look intensifying.

'Heavens, no!' she blurted out, and his sensual lips curved, the cynical half smile tinged with something that seemed a little smug. 'I mean, I never really had feelings for him.' She scrambled to justify her reaction. 'Not *those* feelings, anyway. He's very happily married to my sister Katie. He's a forceful person. And so is Katie, which makes them perfect for each other.'

She took a gulp of the wine, feeling exposed under that patient gaze. Why was she explaining herself to him? Her relationship with Jack—or rather the lack of one—was not his business.

'So why were you ever engaged to him?' he asked.

She wanted to be outraged at the intrusive question. Tried to feel indignant.

But, before she could find a reply, he hooked a tendril of her hair behind her ear. His thumb glided down her cheek, making her skin sizzle, and then stroked the pulse point in her neck, completely disarming her.

Her breathing gathered painfully in her lungs as he tucked his hand back into his pocket. But the damage was already done.

The proprietary touch should have disturbed her, but all it did was energise her and make her rampaging pulse get wedged between her thighs. Her gaze seemed to be locked with his.

She didn't need his approval, so why did what he thought of her seem to matter so much? Enough for her to search for an answer which wouldn't reveal the humiliating truth—that she had been engaged to Jack Wolfe to please her father.

'I… I don't really know,' she lied. 'Jack asked me and I was hopelessly flattered, so I said yes.'

She looked away from his probing gaze, embarrassed by her not entirely truthful answer. But as she imagined what he might think of her lame response, she became brutally aware of the different paths their lives had taken.

Mason Foxx had never bowed to anyone else's wishes but his own. While she'd always taken the easy option, obeying her father because it had been so much less stressful than standing up to him, the way Katie had done. What would this man think of her, if he knew that about her? A man who, by all accounts, had been given nothing, and fought tooth and nail for every single thing he possessed. While she'd been born into privilege, had been handed everything on a silver platter, and owned virtually nothing of any value.

She planned to change that, had convinced herself that honing her language skills would eventually help her find a way out, but the truth was her life at this point was a mere shadow of what it could have been if she'd been less of a doormat.

He hadn't said anything, hadn't responded to her answer. Maybe because he knew it was a lie.

She stared at the magnificent skyline—the majesty of Tower Bridge, the austere beauty of the Tower of London—and finally confronted the full weight of her own cowardice.

'I knew as soon as I said yes to him, it was a colossal mistake,' she murmured, wanting to be as honest as she could without exposing the sordid truth about her choices. 'I knew Jack would consume me, and I could never make him happy. That I wasn't enough for a man like him.'

She blinked furiously, aware of the pity tears she couldn't let fall—because that would be hopelessly self-indulgent.

She was the only one to blame for her pathetic life, her lack of any concrete achievements. Yes, her father was a bully but she could have escaped him long ago, if she'd had Katie's courage. Or the drive and ambition of Mason Foxx, a man who was determined to make his mark no matter the odds he faced.

She turned to find him watching her—the emerald-green eyes glittering with passion and purpose and an intensity which would have been disturbing if it weren't so… Well, so exciting.

What he saw was the illusion, of course—

of a serene, privileged woman in charge of her own life. Instead of a hopeless fake, in charge of nothing of any significance.

But, for once, Bea wanted to live up to the image, the hype. Maybe if a man like Mason Foxx could see something to admire in her, she could see something to admire too.

'What makes you think you're not enough for any man, Beatrice?' he asked softly, sounding genuinely curious.

*Because I know I'm a fake. But I intend to remedy that. Starting now.*

She placed the half-empty glass of expensive wine on the bar. And met that dark, possessive gaze. She smiled, stupidly touched by his faith in her. Or at least in the illusion. And became mesmerised by the gold shards in his irises which were alight with a promise she now understood.

He could take her places she had never been before, never even wanted to go. If she let go of that frightened girl and embraced the woman she could be. The woman she had always wanted to be.

She lifted on tiptoes to cradle his cheek. His jaw tensed as he sucked in a breath and the day-old stubble rasped deliciously against her palm.

His eyes flared with longing. And the excitement in her gut surged, along with the potent feeling of power. And purpose.

'Would you kiss me again, Mason?' she asked.

Glass shattered as he went to place his wine on the bar and missed.

Triumph echoed through her heart at the thought she had so much more power than she had ever realised.

He clasped her hips in strong hands to drag her closer, until the hard line of his body moulded hers. Her nipples tightened painfully, pressed against his chest, the scent of soap and man intoxicating as it enveloped her.

He tucked a knuckle under her chin and bent his head towards her mouth.

But then he rasped, 'You need to be sure, Princess.' The mocking nickname was like an endearment, his hot breath feathering her cheek. 'Because if I kiss you again, we might not be able to stop.'

She swallowed heavily. It was a warning, one that a frightened girl would once have heeded. She was unleashing something bigger than herself, something she knew nothing about. But in this moment, all his warning did was make the adrenaline spike and the ache in her core become painful.

Mason Foxx wanted her, and she wanted him. That was what mattered now.

So she nodded.

His mouth captured her sob of surrender, his lips firm, seeking and voracious. She opened for him again and let him lead the kiss, but as their tongues tangled she found herself making demands of her own.

The kiss became desperate and all-consuming, but also tender. She drove her fingers into his hair and dragged him closer still—his hunger sending her senses into a tailspin of need.

His hands clasped her bottom, pressing her to him, until she became brutally aware of the thick ridge revealing the effect she had on him, which he couldn't hide.

As they came up for air, his harsh pants matched her ragged sobs.

He swore softly, then boosted her into his arms. 'Wrap your legs around my waist,' he rasped.

She did as he asked, unable to deny the dizzying rush of emotion at the realisation he was protecting her bare feet from the broken glass. She clasped his face, kissed his cheeks, his chin, his forehead, loving the feel of his skin on her lips and the harsh murmur of his breathing.

He carried her down a corridor at the back of the space and entered a huge bedroom.

A vast picture window on the far side looked out across the Thames Estuary towards Rotherhithe and the docks—the view was less romantic but somehow more real than the one at the front of the building.

He put her down and her bare toes sank into thick carpeting.

'I want you naked, Beatrice,' he said, the gruff demand in his voice impossibly seductive.

But the raw request made her hesitate.

No man had ever seen her naked before. She'd always been self-conscious about her body, knowing her boyish figure was at its best displayed in designer couture. Would he be disappointed, appalled even, when he saw her virtually flat chest, her narrow hips, her thin frame? She didn't want to risk all her newfound confidence evaporating before they got to the main event.

But she forced herself to nod. As he reached for her, though, she evaded him.

'I want you naked too,' she said.

Perhaps if they were both naked, she would feel less exposed.

His eyebrows lifted, but then he laughed. 'All right, Princess.' The words were mocking, but when he began to unbutton his shirt, revealing the tattoo of barbed wire that looped around his collarbone, her self-consciousness faded, washed away on a surge of heat.

He stripped off the shirt and flung it away.
*Oh...my.*

If she'd thought the view from the lift had been spectacular, it was nothing compared to the sight of Mason Foxx's naked torso.

Her gaze raked over the defined slabs of muscle, the hair-dusted pecs, the ridges of his six-pack, the muscles which arrowed towards his waistband. And the many small scars and two other tattoos—one crude, one intricate—all evidence of the uncharmed life he'd led.

He flipped open the button on his trousers, revealing a pair of black boxer shorts, but just as the rush of moisture flooded her mouth... and her panties...he paused.

'What are you waiting for?' he said, the teasing note doing nothing to disguise the rasp of urgency. 'I thought we were in this together?'

'Oh, yes. Of course,' she said, the last of her self-consciousness incinerated by that playful, provocative tone. She found the side zip of the designer gown with clumsy fingers, slid it down, then paused as he kicked off his shoes, stripped off his trousers.

'You need some help with that?' he asked as he stepped closer.

She nodded because she couldn't seem to move.

His quick grin was feral as he used one fingertip to edge a strap off one shoulder. She shuddered as he eased the other strap down, and the silky dress slid over her body to pool at her feet. She shivered, but she wasn't cold. Not even close.

He stepped back and cleared his throat. 'You're beautiful, Beatrice,' he murmured, his voice so rich with appreciation and approval she felt beautiful for the first time in her life.

'Your hair...' he said, glancing at the elaborate chignon. 'I've been wanting to mess it up all night.'

She wasn't sure if he was asking her permission, but she nodded anyway, loving the thought of him destroying the hairstyle an exclusive stylist had spent over an hour creating.

He located the first pin, dragged it loose. Then another and another. She sighed when the heavy mass tumbled down.

'Shake it,' he demanded. She did as he asked, letting it bounce off her shoulders, aware of his gaze scorching her face, her collarbone and then dipping to her breasts, confined in the strapless bra.

He did a twirl with his finger. 'Turn around.'

Again, she followed his instruction, spellbound by the desire darkening his eyes.

She focused on his tall shape behind her, reflected in the glass wall, illuminated by the low lighting. She jolted as her bra snapped open, the sound like a gunshot in the quiet room.

He peeled off the lace and threw it away. Large hands cupped her breasts from behind. Rough calluses stroked over her engorged flesh, making it tighten and swell. She arched into his touch as firm lips captured the throbbing pulse in her neck. His fingers plucked at her tender nipples, and a ragged moan burst out.

She had never realised she was so sensitive there. But he seemed to know just how to caress and entice her, to drive her passion to fever-pitch as she writhed against his hold.

Too much and yet not enough.

'Look at yourself, Beatrice,' he said, his voice hoarse, his desire as urgent and fierce as her own.

She stared at the woman in the glass, shocked by how wild and uninhibited she seemed, as his hand left her naked breast to glide down her torso. She noticed the bird of prey etched on the back, became mesmerised by the design as his fingers slid into her panties and found the slick folds of her sex.

'You're so wet for me, Beatrice,' he said.

'Yes.' She bucked against his sure touch, her moan becoming a full-throated groan. Bowing back, she reached up, curling her hand around his neck to anchor herself. Panting now, in gasps of need.

'Please…' she begged as he continued to tease and incite, retreating then returning, tempting her swollen flesh.

He swore softly against her neck, then feasted on the pulse point, his other hand still playing with one engorged nipple.

Arrows of sensation darted down, turning the heat at her core into a raging inferno.

The waves of pleasure built with each pass of his thumb, too close and yet not close enough, each swirl of that devious fingertip taking her to the edge, but retreating before she could reach the peak.

'Oh… God.' She gripped his hair, tugged hard, riding his hand now, desperate to release the tension building at her core, vaguely aware of the spectacle she was making of herself but not able to stop, not even able to care.

She bit into her lip as he found the very heart of her.

'Come for me,' he said.

The pleasure centred in her sex—burning, bright, beautiful—then blew apart, sending her shooting over that high ledge. She cried out as the fierce pleasure crested, caught his grunt of triumph through the hurricane in her ears.

And let herself soar. Just like that bird. At last.

\* \* \*

Fierce need enveloped Mason as he scooped Beatrice's limp body into his arms and carried her to the bed.

Had he ever made love to a woman before who was so responsive to his touch? He didn't think so. He had always considered himself skilled at bringing women to climax. He liked sex. A lot. But having her reach for him, feeling the sting as she'd grabbed a fistful of his hair and let herself shatter had been something else…

Urgency charged through his veins, the ache in his groin painful as he laid her out and watched her eyelids flutter open.

She looked dazed and a little confused.

'Hey there,' he said, the emotion scraping against his throat shocking him. 'You okay?'

'Yes. Absolutely,' she said simply. Then she smiled, that sweet, mesmerising, weirdly innocent smile that brightened her whole face and made her look young, in a way he was sure he'd never been.

Her transparent joy and the sense of achievement in her expression made him feel as if he'd just taken her somewhere she'd never been before. Which *had* to be his ego talking, but, even so, he couldn't ignore the swelling against his ribs, or the powerful press of the erection stretching his boxers.

He needed to finish this before he lost what was left of his mind.

'Hold that thought,' he said, forcing an easy smile to his lips that he didn't remotely feel.

He hooked her panties, eased the scrap of lace down long slender legs and breathed in the musty scent of her arousal. Standing, he stared down at her lean body, the small but perfect breasts, the cascade of hair which halloed around her striking face. She was staring back at him, the flush of awareness turning to...

What was that? Because it almost looked like embarrassment.

But then she glanced pointedly at his boxers. 'I thought we agreed we were in this together?' she said in an unsteady voice, despite the snark.

He chuckled, her audacity easing the tension in his chest. Why was he making this a big deal?

'Fair point, Princess,' he said as he dragged off his boxers and threw them away.

Her eyes widened and the unyielding erection swelled as the last of the blood drained out of his head.

Women had looked at him before and commented on his size, usually with appreciation. But when those wide blue eyes met his again and her teeth chewed her bottom lip, he thought he saw panic flit across her features.

Okay. *Unexpected.*

Did she think he was some kind of brute? That he wouldn't treat her with the care and attention she deserved?

He dismissed the thought, shoved it back into the box marked 'newly discovered inferiority complex' and climbed onto the bed, remembering at the last minute to reach into the bedside table. He'd never brought any of his dates here because this was his home base, so he was more than a little relieved when he found a condom.

He ripped open the foil envelope with his teeth then sheathed himself, frantic to get back to where they'd been moments before, when she'd come apart in his arms, before he'd had to worry about practicalities.

He lay down and stroked her cheek, then leant forward to devour those plump lips again. She lifted into his kiss, responding to him eagerly. And the panic receded, to be replaced by pride, smugness even, and pure unadulterated lust.

This was good, this was right. They had incredible chemistry. That was all. No biggie. A connection he intended to enjoy before she left in the morning. But they had a whole night to indulge themselves.

Even so, the desire to rush overwhelmed him

as he reached down to find her ready for him. She bucked against his touch, her gasp one of surprise and surrender, which was more than enough to make his hunger spike.

'Can I touch you too?' she asked as he caressed her, her voice thick with arousal, but still oddly hesitant.

'You don't have to ask for permission,' he managed, touched by the request.

But when she nodded, then reached down to curl slender fingers around his thick shaft, her touch was devastatingly intense even through the condom, and he realised his mistake.

As she stroked him, her caresses somehow both clumsy and bold, the climax built at the base of his spine, threatening to rage out of control... He could only stand it for a few seconds before he grasped her wrist and tugged her fingers away.

'I need to be inside you, Beatrice.'

'Oh... Okay,' she said.

He nodded, then rolled on top of her and grasped her hips in his hands to angle her pelvis. 'Lift your knees,' he groaned as she grasped his shoulders.

He probed at her entrance and held her firmly to press home in one hard thrust.

She tensed, her fingernails digging into his shoulders. And he stopped abruptly. He

groaned, the feel of her—so tight, so exquisite—almost more than he could bear. But had
she just winced?

She was trembling and panting—but, as his
own pleasure built, he could see hers slipping
away.

'Am I hurting you?' he asked, determined
not to move until he was sure, clinging to the
last threads of his control. 'You're so tight,' he
managed as he struggled to hold off the urge to
drive deeper.

He wasn't a small man, he knew that, which
was why he was always careful. But with her
maybe he hadn't been careful enough.

Shame washed over him as he waited, still
lodged inside her, aware of her muscles con-
tracting around him as she struggled to adjust.

'Look at me, Beatrice,' he demanded, his
hand shaking as he cupped her cheek. 'Are you
good?'

She met his gaze at last. 'Yes,' she said. But
he didn't believe her entirely.

Her pupils had dilated to black, a sure sign
of her arousal, but he could see the shock too.
And feel the tension.

Moving his hand, he dragged it down her
torso to locate the place where they joined, determined to bring her pleasure back. She jerked
as he rubbed the hot nub.

'Shh,' he soothed, stroking, inciting, watching as her face began to relax. The tight clasp of her body softened as she relaxed enough to allow him to sink to the hilt.

He gave them both a moment to absorb the sweet shock, but he couldn't control the urge to move for long.

He rose up, adjusting her hips so his pelvis would rub her clitoris on each thrust. He heard her soft pants as the pleasure built again, flowing towards him in furious waves.

She clung to him, her fingers slipping on his shoulders, her panting breaths spurring him on as the coil at the base of his spine tightened, the exquisite sensations furious and raw.

He thrust harder, faster, and she matched his moves, riding into the storm with him.

The wave slammed into him just as her body clenched around his, the climax exploding through him and into her. He threw back his head, the shout one of fury and pleasure beyond bearing as the mind-blowing orgasm crashed over him. He rode the furious wave, pumping everything he was, everything he had into her as he felt her shatter too.

# CHAPTER THREE

*Wow.*

Bea floated in a pool of bliss as Mason collapsed on top of her with his erection still firm, still huge inside her.

Her lungs heaved as she began to swim towards full consciousness—and she became more aware of all the places her body ached.

She felt… New. Different somehow. More sensual, more aware, braver, bolder. And more herself at last.

Or was that just the afterglow?

She focused on a pinprick of red light winking on the ceiling. Peering past Mason's muscular shoulder, she spotted a plane flying across the night sky before it disappeared, probably on its way to City Airport.

The inane observation dragged her the rest of the way out of her blissful bubble and into uncomfortable reality.

She gave Mason a soft shove, then flinched

when he moved off her... Moved *out* of her. A moan escaped.

He rose over her, his expression difficult to decipher in the shadows, but she heard his uneasiness when he cradled her cheek.

'What's wrong? Did I hurt you?'

She shook her head, foolish tears stinging her eyelids. She covered his hand and dragged it away from her face, terrified by the emotion swelling in her throat.

It *had* hurt, a little bit, at first. She had no yardstick to measure him against, but she was pretty sure he was not your average guy. She guessed it stood to reason given his height. She'd actually been quite worried when she'd seen that prodigious erection in all its glory for the first time.

But he had been so careful with her, so attuned to her distress—something she really hadn't expected. Or been prepared for.

Just like she really hadn't been prepared for how overwhelming it would be, not just having him inside her, but having him give her another, even more powerful release as they'd strained to reach their release together.

Was that why her emotions felt so raw? So wobbly and tender. She'd waited such a long time to have sex, had convinced herself she might never even want it, so the intensity of the orgasms he'd given her had seemed significant. When they really weren't.

His shoulders relaxed and his forehead touched hers. 'Good,' he murmured.

She swallowed, far too aware of his concern for her.

He rolled away and sat on the edge of the bed.

Awareness spread as he stood with his back to her, holding his shorts, then crossed to a door on the other side of the room. She grabbed the sheet to cover herself—suddenly self-conscious—as he switched on the light in the adjoining room. She got a glimpse of a glass shower and quartz tiles—and an eyeful of his magnificent body, and the red marks on his shoulder blades where her nails had dug into his skin. A Celtic design etched across his lower back drew her gaze to his magnificent glutes—and had heat pooling in her abdomen—before he disappeared into the bathroom and shut the door.

She lay on the bed, listening to the water switch on and eventually off.

Her heartbeat was threatening to choke her by the time he finally reappeared—which seemed to take hours.

Thank goodness he had put his boxers on, although she could still make out the outline of his sex—which looked, if not fully erect, then certainly not limp either.

Goodness, was he already interested in doing it again?

He cleared his throat. 'Up here, Beatrice.' Her gaze shot to his face.

His wry tone was belied by the frown on his face. The guilty blush—because he had caught her staring at his crotch—bloomed across her collarbone and flooded her cheeks.

She tried to concentrate on his frown and interpret it as he perched on the bed next to her.

Had he been expecting her to get dressed and leave while he was in the bathroom? She had no idea what the etiquette was for a one-night stand, a hook-up. She sat up abruptly, clasping the sheet to her breasts. Why hadn't she made her getaway while he was showering? Now she looked as clueless and unsophisticated as she actually was.

Time to find her panties and scram.

'I should probably make a move,' she murmured. But as she scooted away from him, he snagged her upper arm.

'Not so fast, Beatrice. I have a question.'

'Oh? Okay,' she said, trying to sound nonchalant, not easy when her face had to be glowing brightly enough to be seen from space and he could probably feel her shaking. 'What…what question?'

'Why didn't you tell me you were a virgin?'

'How did you know?' she blurted out.

Then wanted to slap herself when his gaze sharpened. Why hadn't she lied, played dumb?

She felt so exposed now, the sheet doing nothing to hide the blush, which had exploded.

'I guessed,' he said, letting go of her arm. 'So, it's true. I'm the first guy you've ever slept with.'

She wanted desperately to lie, but how could she when she'd totally outed herself already? Anyway, wouldn't lying make her seem even more unsophisticated?

'Well…yes. But it's really not a big deal,' she said, although of course it was.

Awkward, much. Could she actually seem more clueless and immature?

'Why me?' he asked, his voice gentle but his gaze acute.

'I just… I just wasn't ready before. But with you…' She hesitated.

If only she knew what he was thinking. Was he annoyed? Freaked out? Embarrassed for her? Did he think the fact she'd waited so long, to then do it with a man she barely knew was sad, or funny, or simply pathetic?

It was impossible to tell, because his expression was completely unreadable.

'But with me… What?' he prompted.

She turned away from his probing gaze. The stunning view of the Docklands—laid out before them like a carpet of wonders—did nothing to make her feel any less silly and insignificant.

He took her chin in his hand to turn her face to his.

'Out with it, Beatrice. I want to know why you didn't sleep with the guy you were engaged to, but you slept with me.'

She heard it then, the edge in his voice.

Why was he so interested in her engagement to Jack Wolfe, when it felt about a million years ago now?

Although she supposed he did have a point. She wasn't sure she had an answer for him though. Not a coherent one anyway, because she didn't really know *why* she'd been so eager to leap into his arms this evening—when she'd never been reckless or impulsive or even turned on really, by Jack or any other guy, until now.

If only she knew why Mason looked so wary and tense.

He'd stopped calling her Princess. Even though she'd disliked the nickname at first, she missed it now. Because it had seemed light and teasing and affectionate, even if he had been mocking her. And for a moment it had made her feel like his equal.

She stared at her hands, the knuckles whitening as she clutched the sheet.

She'd never felt more powerless in her life.

And that was saying quite a lot, considering she'd been under her father's thumb for most of it.

She shrugged, but the movement felt brittle and stiff. 'I guess with you I felt safe.'

Which sounded ludicrous when she said it out loud. But he didn't laugh at her, which was something.

'And really turned on,' she continued.

If she was going to tell him the truth she might as well tell him the whole truth, even if the blush rising up her neck was liable to set fire to her cheeks any second. 'There's a reason they called me the Ice Queen. And that's the reason, right there.'

His frown became a fissure. 'I don't get it—what reason?'

'I'm basically frigid.' She pushed the words out.

But, instead of agreeing with her, his dark brows rose, and then he laughed. 'Hell, Beatrice, I don't know who told you that…or who *they* are…' His gaze skated over her, making her skin prickle. 'But they're wrong. I've never met anyone hotter or more responsive.'

'Really?' she said, stupidly pleased with his verdict, even though it made her look like even more of a fool.

He cupped her cheek, clasped her neck to pull

her towards him, then dropped his forehead to hers. She could hear him breathing. Feel the tension in him rising as her own body melted in response. That delicious, provocative, exciting tension which they'd released together so spectacularly less than ten minutes ago.

'Yeah, really,' he muttered, then he kissed her.

The kiss was gentle but also possessive. Her heart thundered, the relief making her light-headed.

Whatever had just happened, he didn't despise her and he wasn't angry with her…

He broke off the kiss, but his thumb continued to stroke the pulse hammering against her collarbone, making her aware of the heat pooling between her thighs, but also the discomfort.

'I'm honoured that you chose me,' he said, surprising her not just with the blunt statement, but also the way it made the ache in her ribs increase. 'Would you like to stay tonight?'

She nodded because she was finding it hard to speak.

She was unbearably touched by his candid admission, especially as she suspected he wasn't a man who revealed his feelings easily. Or would admit to being honoured very often.

'Do you want to grab a shower?' he asked.

She nodded again. He found a robe in the wardrobe, which dwarfed her when she put it on. But she was grateful for the chance to cover her nakedness, feeling self-conscious again as she darted into the bathroom.

She took her time—trying not to think about the way her heart was all but choking her.

His reaction wasn't what she'd expected. At all. He'd been perceptive and understanding when she had expected him to be appalled—making her glad she'd chosen to trust him with her first time.

When she returned to the bedroom he was stretched out on the bed, looking hot and delicious and… Her gaze snagged on the pronounced ridge in his boxer shorts. *Dangerous.*

'I'm not sure I can do it again tonight,' she admitted, even as the heat surged. 'I'm a bit sore.'

He chuckled, the rough sound alluring.

'Don't worry. We're gonna have to take a rain-check anyway because we have a situation with the condoms. How about I just hold you? You might want to grab a T-shirt from the dresser, though, to stop me getting any ideas.'

'I'd like that.' She grinned, his thoughtfulness making the emotion swell again.

After finding an oversized T-shirt which covered all the essential bits, she climbed onto the bed and he tugged her into his arms. Her body relaxed into the warmth of his and she inhaled the delicious scent of pine soap. But then her mind snagged on something he'd said.

'What's the situation with the condoms?'

His fingers, which were stroking her arm and setting off all kinds of interesting sensations, stopped. He cleared his throat. And she glanced round to find him staring at her.

'Turns out they're older than I thought. You're the first woman I've brought here in…' He shifted slightly, and if she knew him better she might have thought he seemed embarrassed. 'Well, ever, actually. I guess I must have stashed them in the drawer four years ago when I moved in.'

She folded her arms across her chest, rather enjoying his discomfort. After all, didn't they say turnaround was fair play?

'Four years?'

She was the first woman he'd brought here? Why did that feel so significant, and flattering?

'I should have checked the date on them, but I was too desperate to have you…'

She grinned. She couldn't help it—this was getting better and better.

'Okay, well, I guess if we're going to do this again…' She paused, realising she really, *really* wanted to. With him.

They didn't have a future together. They were far too different and she was about to leave the kind of social circles he moved in. Plus, his wealth would be a barrier to the new life she wanted to establish for herself—as an independent, self-sufficient woman. But having just discovered she had a libido, she didn't want to bury it again yet.

'You'll have to buy some new ones,' she finished. 'Or I could?'

'So, you're not on any form of birth control?' he asked, his expression becoming pained.

'Not yet. No.'

'Crap,' he murmured. 'Okay, then we do have a bigger problem. The condom we just used burst.'

Embarrassment flooded her cheeks and she lifted off his chest. Of course, that was what he'd been alluding to. Exactly how stupid was she that she hadn't figured it out sooner?

'It's okay, Beatrice.' He sat up abruptly and grasped her arm. 'Don't panic. Where are you in your cycle?'

She tried to focus on the question, not easy with the crippling embarrassment. 'I had my last period about three weeks ago.'

'That's good,' he said, trying to be reassuring, while all sorts of eventualities were charging into her head now... None of them good.

How could she not have protected herself? Good grief, she hadn't even thought about contraception until he'd produced a condom—a faulty, out-of-date condom.

'You're not right in the middle of your cycle, at least,' he added.

'No, but I could still get pregnant. That's a bit of a myth. Unless one of us is infertile.' Although she could not imagine Mason Foxx firing blanks, and she suspected she was unlikely to be infertile either.

After all, hadn't Katie fallen pregnant after her first encounter with Jack Wolfe? It was why her sister and Jack had had a shotgun wedding only a few months after Bea had broken off her engagement to him.

Of course, Jack and Katie were blissfully happy together now. But it had been really tough for them for a while. And Katie had the kind of guts and fortitude Bea could only dream of. Plus, she couldn't imagine Mason Foxx being happy about becoming an accidental father after a one-night booty call.

But instead of looking worried, he smiled. Was this funny? Because it didn't feel very funny.

'Yeah, I guess it is a myth,' he said. 'But I'm a firm believer in not panicking until there's actually something to panic about. I'll make you an appointment with my doctor tomorrow and we can check out our options, just in case…'

'But what if…?'

He placed his finger over her lips. 'Don't get spooked again, Princess,' he said.

The return of the affectionate nickname soothed her anxiety, a bit.

'We can't figure out anything until morning,' he added. 'But then we can take whatever precautions we need to make sure this is not a problem.'

His calmness, and the way he said *we*—making it clear, however reckless they had been, they were in this together—helped her to relax more.

'Come here,' he said, propping himself against the pillows and dragging her back into his arms.

She allowed herself to be held, the rollercoaster of emotion she'd been on all night catching up with her in a rush.

She guessed that was what losing your virginity, having two titanic orgasms when you thought you were frigid, then discovering you could be accidentally pregnant could do to you…

'We'll figure it out tomorrow, okay? I swear,' he said, his voice forceful and so reassuring it made her heart hurt.

Of course, they had options. Lots of options. This didn't have to be a catastrophe.

She nodded against his chest. She shouldn't rely on him too much. But, just for tonight, would it be so wrong to bow to his pragmatism? To let him take charge?

'Now, go to sleep, you're exhausted,' he added.

'I know…' she said, cracking a huge yawn. 'You exhausted me.'

She closed her eyes, feeling at least a little bit kickass again when his rough chuckle lured her to sleep.

# CHAPTER FOUR

MASON SPRINTED UP the building's back staircase in his running gear, his headphones blaring out a favourite R&B classic and the fresh pastries he'd bought at the bakery round the corner slung under his arm.

But despite the three-mile run he'd taken all the way to the London Eye and back along the Embarkment, endorphins were still rioting through his system. Because one of the most captivating women he'd ever met was lying in his bed, waiting for him—after a night of insanely good sex.

Insanely good, even though she had been a virgin. He slowed to a jog as he reached the top floor, then shoved open the fire door with his shoulder—still not one hundred percent sure how he felt about that.

When he'd first figured out the truth in the bathroom, while also discovering the condom he'd used wasn't fit for purpose, he'd been stunned.

Why would a woman like Beatrice—classy, beautiful and more sensitive than he'd first realised—choose a man like him? He was hardly known for his sensitivity. Nor did he have a great track record when it came to relationships.

He wasn't a guy who had ever worn his heart on his sleeve. If he even had a heart any more...

He'd jettisoned the need for love a long time ago—and he didn't regret it. Because it had made him tougher and more resilient. His emotional self-sufficiency, the ability to trust in his own judgement, had helped him to build a multi-billion-pound global hospitality brand in the space of a decade.

But when she'd blurted out the truth, confirming his suspicions about her lack of experience, instead of being annoyed, or wary, or freaked out, what had surged up his torso had felt a lot like pride. It was the same feeling of validation he remembered from the day he'd signed the lease on his first property—a crumbling bedsit in Hoxton which he'd rehabbed himself over one long hot summer and turned into his first boutique hotel—at the age of twenty-one.

He'd never quite managed to replicate that spurt of fierce joy and pride in his accomplishments—until he'd woken up this morning, with

Beatrice curled around him, fast asleep, wearing one of his old T-shirts. Her breath had feathered his collarbone, her scent—vanilla and female arousal—had filled his lungs and his body had been raring to go again in seconds.

Hence the need for a three-mile run.

He didn't know why she'd trusted him with something so precious, but he was glad she had. It had stunned him, but it had also humbled him…in a way he hadn't been humbled in a long time. And while he was still grappling with the fallout from her decision—and why it had affected him so deeply—one thing he was sure of. He didn't want to let her go. Not yet.

He took a deep breath and ignored the constriction in his chest.

*Okay, Foxx, get real. This is just about the insanely good sex—and your gargantuan ego.*

If he didn't do love, he sure as hell didn't do love after one night.

He walked into the apartment's open-plan living space and took a moment to admire the way the spring sunshine gleamed off the expensive furniture a world-class interior designer had spent a fortune selecting for him and sparkled on the water outside.

As the mighty Thames snaked through the magnificent view, the light feeling in his chest refused to subside.

He had a good life. A great life. A life he'd spent seventeen years working like a dog to create for himself. But until last night, when Beatrice had fallen asleep in his arms and that odd feeling of possessiveness had settled into his gut, it had never even occurred to him there could be more. That maybe he'd spent so much of his life striving to achieve the next milestone on his journey to world domination of the hospitality industry, he'd never taken the time to create something which couldn't be bought and paid for.

Until last night, he had never valued anything he couldn't put a price on. But her trust in him meant something. Even if he wasn't entirely sure what.

He placed the fresh pastries on a plate and walked to the main bedroom to check on her. Her slight shape lay curled under the duvet on the far side of his bed—had she even moved? Boy, he really had exhausted her last night.

His ribs tightened again, even as his heartbeat plunged into his shorts.

He headed to the guest bedroom to shower and change so he wouldn't wake her. After washing away the sweat from his run, he switched the dial to frigid to get himself under control.

She was going to be sore this morning. Which

meant there was going to be no repeat performance, however much he might want one. But his disappointment—at the thought he was going to have to wait to make love to her again—faded at the thought of getting the chance to talk to her.

Because there were so many things he wanted to know about her.

She'd been more candid than he'd expected about her engagement to Wolfe. He could admit now he had been wildly jealous of that previous attachment—another new experience for him. But the green-eyed monster had died as soon as he'd discovered she'd never let Wolfe make love to her.

He grinned. *Neanderthal, or what?*

After tugging on a pair of sweats and a T-shirt, he grabbed his work mobile off the chest of drawers, to discover numerous messages from his PA Joe McCarthy and more from Jackson White, the head of the PR company he used to manage the Foxx Group's public profile. After a cursory glance, he clicked through to a tabloid article attached to one of Jackson's messages—and winced at the cheesy headline: *Has Hotel Hottie Foxx Melted the Medford Ice Queen?*

Then he enlarged the shot of him and Beatrice leaving the club the night before which illustrated the piece. He chuckled, because apparently nothing was going to sour his good mood this morning.

Not bad, he decided. They looked good together, with her cradled in his arms as if she belonged there. Jackson had attached the screenshot of the article to a message which simply read:

WTH Mace?! We need to talk about your new girlfriend.

*Cheeky sod.*

But then he and Jackson went way back, to the early days.

He'd catch up with him later today because Beatrice wasn't his girlfriend. *Yet.* But Jackson's question had him picturing her on his arm for the social events he usually found a major chore. His heart bobbed in his chest at the realisation she would make those boring events a lot more entertaining. The fact that her classy beauty would not do the Foxx brand any harm at all was not lost on him either.

*Getting way ahead of yourself again, bro.*

He dialled his PA, because before he and Beatrice had a conversation about their future he needed to make her an appointment with his doctor as he'd promised.

As he waited for Joe to pick up—because it was still only seven a.m. on a Saturday—he realised he was surprisingly ambivalent about the possibility of an unplanned pregnancy. Of course, they had a lot of options if his condom *faux pas* led to that. But even after he'd discovered the tear in the condom last night—something which would have bothered him big time with any of the other women he'd dated—the panic hadn't come.

Children weren't on his radar. Never had been. He really wasn't the paternal type. What did he even know about family, or being a dad, when his mum had done a runner when he was still little more than a baby and his old man had been such a loser? But when he'd confronted Beatrice with the problem and she'd panicked, he'd been surprisingly calm—and weirdly turned on—because he couldn't quite get past the delicious thought of Beatrice's slender body round with his child.

He closed his eyes briefly as a renewed surge of desire fired through his system.

'Hey Mason.' Joe picked up at last. 'How are you? I didn't expect to hear from you this morning. Especially after who you pulled last night.' Joe let out a wry laugh, because he was also a mate. 'How was the Medford Ice Queen? Not too chilly, I hope,' he added, still with that teasing tone.

Mason frowned, not liking it, or the nickname which couldn't have been further from the truth. And which he had begun to suspect had left Beatrice with a ton of hang-ups.

'Don't call her that, Joe.'

'All right. No problem, bro,' Joe replied, the jokey tone sobering.

'Actually, I need you to contact Dr Lee. Make an appointment for Beatrice today. Out of hours.'

He trusted the people he employed to keep his business confidential. But after last night's headlines he needed to protect Beatrice from any more unwanted attention while they were figuring out their relationship. Perhaps he could persuade her to fly with him to New York tomorrow night? On Monday he was due to start scoping out sites for the Foxx Group to expand into the US, so he could totally make the case for it business-wise. And it would give them a chance to get away from the British media and have a time out to talk about last night. And what they wanted to happen next. He'd never considered having a mistress because he thought the whole concept was tacky and old-fashioned, but he could totally get behind the idea of having Beatrice at his beck and call for a while.

'Okay,' Joe said. 'Can I tell Dr Lee what it's about?'

Mason hesitated. 'Just a standard check-up,' he prevaricated. Then wondered why he was prevaricating. There was nothing wrong with taking responsibility for the burst condom. 'Plus, we need to discuss birth control options. And get Beatrice a pregnancy test.'

Joe gasped, then cursed. 'So you *did* thaw out the Ice Queen. That's fast work, even for you.'

'I thought I told you not to call her that,' Mason said, annoyed.

'Yeah, but… Mase…' Joe sounded concerned, which seemed like a massive overreaction. 'Are you sure you want to date her for real?'

'What's that supposed to mean?' he asked, his happy buzz turning into genuine irritation. Did everyone have an opinion on his sex life? And Beatrice's. No wonder she had so many hang-ups.

'You do know her old man has targeted you as a possible son-in-law?'

'What?' he murmured, irritation turning to shock as the happy buzz he'd woken up with imploded.

'Medford. It's not that big a secret he's been looking to hook his youngest daughter up with an advantageous match for years. It's why she was engaged to Wolfe a while back. Rumour is Wolfe lent him a ton of money, then swallowed the loss when he got hitched to the older sister and broke it off with Beatrice. She does what her old man wants, unlike Katherine.'

Mason sank down onto the edge of the bed, his knees too shaky to hold him. So many thoughts and feelings were bombarding him he couldn't seem to differentiate any of them. Except the hole opening up in the pit of his stomach, which he remembered from when he was a kid.

He cut off the memories.

Not going there. Not ever. That was ancient history. He'd been a skinny boy back then, still kidding himself his mum would come back one day and his dad wasn't a bad guy, just a man with an addiction he couldn't control.

But he wasn't that gullible, stupid kid any more, had stopped being him when he'd left that life behind.

He thrust his fingers through his hair, appalled to realise his hand was shaking. He clenched his fingers into a fist to stop the pathetic reaction. And noticed the phoenix in flight he'd had inked onto the back of his hand when he was fourteen years old. The night he'd promised never to let anyone use him again.

'What makes you think Medford has *me* targeted as a possible son-in-law?' he asked, surprised his voice was steady when his stomach was so jumpy he felt nauseous.

Was that why she had chosen him? To take her virginity. It had never been about him, or the livewire sexual connection he had thought was genuine... She had never really been into him. She'd been told to come on to him by her old man.

'Just stuff I've heard in the last few days,' Joe said, sounding increasingly uncomfortable. 'When I saw the pictures online last night, of you and her leaving the Cascade launch, I figured you knew. That you were playing her.'

So last night had been a big fat lie that he'd fallen for. Enough to be all bright-eyed and bushy-tailed this morning at the thought of dating her. Of making her his.

'I'm not that desperate to get laid, Joe,' he said, but he could hear the bitterness in his own voice. And the shame.

Because he was exactly that desperate. Or why would he have fallen for her act so easily? He'd even told her he had been honoured she'd chosen him to be her first, like some romantic fool. Instead of a man who had always known the score. That women like her thought they were above guys like him.

Which was really ironic. Because, for all her airs and graces and that plummy accent, she was no better than the women who used to leave their calling cards in the broken phone boxes around Bermondsey when he was a boy. The big difference being those women hadn't had a choice. Had been driven by desperation, poverty, coercion and/or addiction. He'd always had sympathy for them. He had no sympathy for Beatrice Medford, though. Because she hadn't been forced to play him last night. She probably thought she was better than those working girls too, except she wasn't. Because she wasn't desperate, she was just spoilt and entitled. And greedy.

'Right. Well, thanks for letting me know,' Mason murmured.

'You still want me to make that appointment with Dr Lee?'

He frowned. And swore softly.

Hell, she could be pregnant. Had she planned that too? Maybe not. After all, he was the one who had supplied the faulty condom. But she hadn't even mentioned birth control. Her panic last night must have been an act too, he decided. Because surely a pregnancy would fit right in with her father's get-your-hooks-into-Mason agenda.

And if she were pregnant he would be stuck

with her, because one thing he would never do was desert his own flesh and blood, the way his mother had.

'Yes,' he said, thrusting his fingers through his hair, his anger at her and himself—for being such a chump—starting to consume him. 'But tell Lee I'll want her to persuade Ms Medford to agree to a pregnancy test ASAP.'

If there were consequences, he would deal with them. His way.

He ended the call with Joe, then sat staring at the view he'd been so proud of five minutes ago—the view which had assured him he had finally arrived, and had become the man he had always wanted to be. Not just successful, but worthy of success.

The view which now looked flat and dull and ostentatious.

Because he'd just been taken for a colossal mug. By Beatrice *and* her old man.

But even as he nursed his resentment and nurtured his fury—so he could fill up the hole in his gut—an empty space remained.

Reminding him there was still some of that dumb kid inside him—the kid who could be hurt. The kid he thought he'd killed a lifetime ago. The little boy who had waited for his mum to return for months, until he'd finally wised up and realised she was never coming back. But somehow Beatrice Medford had found that kid and exploited him.

'Hi, Mason, are you here?' her voice called from the living room, shy and unsure.

He forced himself to get off the bed.

He spotted her standing by the coffee machine as he walked into the living area. And had to brace against the visceral jolt of heat. How could he still want her? When she had played him so comprehensively.

But when she swung round and he saw the vivid blush slashing across her cheeks and the shy smile lifting lips still red from last night's kisses, he knew exactly why. Wearing nothing but the old T-shirt which skimmed her thighs and showed off her mile-long legs to perfection, her hair a mess of unruly curls and her ragged breathing drawing his gaze to the way her unfettered breasts peaked beneath the worn cotton, she looked so fresh and appealing and guileless his mouth watered.

Cynical fury twisted inside him as he rode the wave of want. Because it was fake.

Or mostly fake. Their livewire connection had been real, because she sure as hell hadn't faked those orgasms. But she had also bartered her virginity and risked a pregnancy to hook him.

Somehow, though, as the fury engulfed him,

the possibility didn't seem like a total disaster any more. Maybe there would be benefits from having Beatrice Medford on his arm for a price. At least he wouldn't have to deal with all the hearts and flowers nonsense.

On his arm she could give him a class he'd always secretly yearned for. And while he'd never seriously considered becoming a father, he had thought vaguely about his legacy. And about one day, in the distant future, passing it on.

If that time turned out to be now, who better to spruce up his bloodline than the daughter of a lord?

And, best of all, he'd be in control. Because he had something she and her father needed. Money. And now he knew the truth about her, she wouldn't be able to dynamite that stupid kid out of hiding a second time.

'Good morning, Princess,' he said, careful to keep the edge out of his voice as he climbed onto a stool at the breakfast bar. The endearment which had been a joke last night wasn't really a joke any more, though.

He sent her one of his fake smiles, the kind he used when he wanted to lull the competition into thinking he was all charm and no substance.

'How you doing this morning?' he asked, pouring on the bad-boy-made-good schtick, even though he felt empty inside.

So what if their relationship would be just another transaction? All that mattered now was that, like all the other deals he'd made in his life, he came out on top.

'Good, thank you,' Bea said politely as she noticed the tattoo which roped around Mason's biceps and flexed under the short sleeve of his T-shirt. And tried not to notice the wobble in her stomach, which had been getting worse ever since she'd woken up in his bed, feeling warm and languid and well-rested.

That would be the wobble which had just gone into overdrive when he had strolled towards her in jogging bottoms and a T-shirt, with his feet bare and his damp hair raked into haphazard rows.

In the daylight, the expensive, starkly modern apartment and the devastating view of Tower Bridge looked even more intimidating... But nowhere near as intimidating as the man himself—her lover—in his natural habitat.

She took a careful breath, aware of his glittering green gaze roaming over her face... Except... What had happened to the warmth from last night? Why did the look in his eyes suddenly seem a little impatient?

Perhaps he hadn't expected her to still be here? Should she have left already? Unfortunately, she knew even less about morning-after etiquette than she did about one-night stand etiquette.

But something was definitely off. Because the Princess endearment seemed less like an endearment now too. And she was sure she could detect the sparkle of resentment in his gaze.

But perhaps that was just her insecurity? The insecurity which had stopped her living her best life—or any life at all really—for so long.

She forced herself to smile and crossed her arms over her chest. She wished she had found something less revealing to wear before she'd walked out here in search of coffee... And him. But it was too late to stress about that.

Things had become far too heavy last night, thanks to her virginity and his busted condom. But she didn't want to appear anxious or nervous, or as if she was expecting some kind of commitment. Because she really wasn't.

He probably already thought she was clueless and gauche and over-sensitive. So she needed to bring her A-game now and create a much better impression. She wanted to appear smart and empowered and worldly—and not as if her emotions were all over the place, even if they were.

But for that, she definitely needed coffee.

She turned her attention to his state-of-the-art espresso machine. 'I'm afraid I may need a degree in nuclear physics to figure out how to work this.'

'I'll do it,' he said. 'I guess you're not used to making your own coffee.'

She heard the note of judgement, but was certain that *had* to be her projecting.

He joined her by the machine, but as she stepped aside to give him room—far too aware of his scent—he gave a rough chuckle.

'Why so jumpy, Princess?' he asked.

She glanced at him, the heat exploding in her cheeks—because she'd definitely heard an edge this time, as if he found her nervous reaction vaguely pathetic.

'I'm… I'm not,' she stuttered, as the wobble stamped around in her stomach like a jumping bean wearing hobnailed boots.

'Sure you are,' he said with a certainty which made her feel embarrassed about her lie. 'How about we try this?' he added, then leaned back against the countertop. Placing a hand on her waist, he tugged her between his outstretched thighs.

She braced her hands on his chest. Her gaze was level with the tantalising ring of barbed wire on his collarbone, her lungs full of the smell of him, fresh from the shower—sandalwood and pine soap. But while his scent had been intoxicating the night before, it bothered her that she couldn't control her reaction to it. Not just the surge of endorphins, but also the nerves playing havoc with the booted jumping bean in her belly.

He lifted her chin, forcing her to meet that assessing, pragmatic gaze. He placed a kiss on her nose, the gesture just casual enough to be condescending.

'There's no need to be nervous. I'm happy to take a rain check before round two, Princess.'

She stiffened. She wished he would stop calling her that. She didn't like it any more. Because the nickname seemed to be loaded with the brittle cynicism she'd noticed when he'd first stepped into her path at the club, but had convinced herself had never been aimed at her. Now she was a lot less sure.

'What makes you think round two is a foregone conclusion?' she murmured, finally getting up the courage to assert herself, at least a little bit.

'Yeah? Why wouldn't it be?' The penetrating gaze skated over her—kicking off those blasted endorphins again—but she didn't feel confident and empowered any more, she felt hopelessly exposed... And unfairly judged. 'Is it because I haven't proposed marriage yet?' he added, his voice thick with derision now. 'Or because you need to let Daddy know you've got me on the hook first before you put out again?'

Her jaw dropped as she lurched out of his arms, not sure she'd heard him correctly. Or understood what he was implying.

'I'm sorry, what did you say?' she managed to murmur around the boulder in her throat.

He laughed again, but the caustic chuckle held no humour at all.

'Come on, Princess, you can drop the act now. I know why the Medford Ice Queen deigned to jump me last night. The virginity was a nice touch, by the way—cute and original. And I'll admit the condom was my bad, although I'm sure we can figure out a way to make any consequences work for both of us. But I'm not as dumb as you seem to think I am. Nor am I as gullible or as easily impressed as Jack Wolfe.'

She stumbled back another step, so horrified she couldn't breathe, couldn't even really process what he had just said. There were so many unfair and unjust accusations to unpick, she couldn't seem to grasp hold of any of them.

But what was far worse was the way he was looking at her... As if she were...*nothing*. Because the cruel resentment and the rigid fury in his gaze threw her back to that terrible night when her father had ranted and raved and thrown Katie out of the house. Then turned to her and told her to stop whimpering and get out of his sight.

And she'd done exactly what he'd told her.

But Mason's ruthless demolition of her confidence was so much worse because, instead of shouting or screaming, he looked so calm, so cold, so confident. And, unlike her father, who had never been able to control his temper, Mason knew exactly how much damage he was doing.

'Okay,' she said calmly, without any clue as to why she was so calm when he had just sliced apart her self-esteem in a few scalpel-sharp strokes like a surgeon extracting a donor's heart, each cut deeper and more efficient than the last.

But this was no bloodless evisceration, she realised as soon as she managed to gather enough oxygen for her lungs to start functioning again, because the injury felt all too real.

She walked into the bedroom on autopilot. After discarding his T-shirt, she found her dress and yanked it on, then located her shoes, all as the suffocating memories from that night so long ago—and from last night—pressed down on the gaping wound in her chest.

The only thing that mattered now was getting out of here before the pain became too debilitating.

'I should go,' she said, again with perfect politeness, as she crossed the living room.

He stood by the counter, staring at her as if she had lost her mind. But it was a sign of how far gone she was that his cynical frown seemed like a win compared to the blank indifference of moments before.

'So, you're going to sulk now? Because I figured out your little act?' he asked.

She didn't reply, because it took all her strength to keep putting one foot in front of the other. Once she got out of the loft apartment she dashed to the emergency stairs, knowing she couldn't wait for the lift in case he followed her.

She had to hold it together, had to get out.

But as she scrambled down the stairwell she couldn't hold back the indescribable pain any longer. Or the silent, self-pitying tears, so reminiscent of the night when she had watched her sister being evicted from her life... And done nothing.

She scrubbed her cheeks, sucking in jerky breaths, the vague thought circling around and around in her head that these tears were just as futile and pointless and cowardly now as they had been when she was twelve. When her world had fallen apart the first time.

# CHAPTER FIVE

'HELLO, MRS GOULDING, is my sister at home?' Bea bit into her lip, determined to hold back the crying jag which had demolished her during the cab journey from Tower Bridge to Katie and Jack's house in Mayfair.

Clare Goulding, her sister's housekeeper, was a professional, so her expression barely changed as she took in Bea's bedraggled appearance. But Bea could see the pity in the older woman's eyes when she replied.

'Why, yes. Mr and Mrs Wolfe are in the dining room having breakfast with Luca. Do come in.' She held the door wide, not asking for an explanation. 'I'll let them know you're here.'

'Thank you, but could I borrow some money first to pay the cab driver who brought me here?' Shame washed over her at the thought of the cabbie she had begged a lift.

'I'll handle it, Miss Beatrice,' the housekeeper said. 'Don't worry.'

Guilt twisted in Bea's stomach, adding to the wave of humiliation which had been building ever since she had run out of Mason Foxx's penthouse loft half an hour ago.

Panic had assailed her in the cab, finally drying the futile tears as she'd realised she couldn't return to her father's house or everything Mason had accused her of would be true.

Maybe she had been driven by an attraction, an excitement which had been totally real to her as Mason had kissed and caressed and eventually possessed her last night. But how could she claim to be her own woman, able to make her own decisions, when sleeping with Mason had also been what her father wanted?

She wanted to hate Mason for pretending to care about her, even a little bit, the night before. Because it had brought back all the old yearnings—to matter to someone, to be special and cherished, the way she could vaguely remember her Welsh granny had once cherished her... But did she really have the right to be angry that Mason wasn't who he had pretended to be when she wasn't either? And, frankly, what had she ever done to deserve to be cherished by anyone, anyhow?

Mason Foxx had just said this morning what everyone else already knew but were too polite to say. She was a parasite.

'I'm sure Mr and Mrs Wolfe will be overjoyed to see you,' the housekeeper added, scooping up her purse from the side table. She headed out to pay for Bea's cab.

*Will they? Why?*

Bea stood dumbly in the lobby, wanting desperately to run down the hall and recount all the cruel things Mason Foxx had said and done, then cry on Katie's shoulder and let her big sister make it all better somehow.

As she had done so many times before.

Because whenever Bea had screwed up, whenever she needed a respite from their father's demands and ultimatums, or whenever she just needed a fix of her adorable nephew Luca, she would rush over here and let Katie comfort and console her and make her feel better about herself and her refusal to do anything concrete to change her life.

How would this time really be any different?

The sound of Luca's giggles, followed by the rumble of Jack's deep voice and her sister's laughter filtered from the room down the hall. Yearning ripped through Bea's chest, but right behind it was disgust, with herself and her selfishness.

She should not have come here.

Jack and Katie both had busy careers which made their quality time with their son Luca incredibly precious. Not only that, but Katie was in the first trimester of her second pregnancy, and Bea knew her sister was suffering again from morning sickness. She would never turn Bea away. But what right did Bea have to add to her sister's responsibilities, to ask her to fix another of the stupid mistakes Bea had made, when all Bea's problems were entirely of her own making?

Seeing Katie's gym bag beside the hall table, she grabbed it.

She needed a change of clothing, and while Katie and she were hardly the same shape, they *were* the same shoe size. She scribbled out a note on the pad in the hall, apologising for borrowing the clothes and promising to pay Katie back. Then she forced herself to add the sentence she should have written years ago.

*I've decided to leave London. Thank you for all your support over the years, but I've finally got this now.*
*Love B x*

Maybe if she wrote it down, she could begin to believe it.

She could still hear Jack's and Katie's voices, and their son Luca giggling, as she headed out of the house, her guilt and humiliation joined by misery and panic.

A part of her knew the reason she wanted to leave London and disappear wasn't just because she couldn't continue to lean on her sister, but also because Mason Foxx lived here.

*Strike two to Bea the coward!*

The hope, the bubble of confidence, the excitement and exhilaration at her own boldness last night, had never been anything other than desire. She understood that now. Mason hadn't needed to be so cruel. But she was the one who had wilfully believed a fairy tale. She was the one who had let him hurt her—because she had once again been looking to someone else to give her life substance and meaning.

Her heart tore in her chest as she walked down the front steps, leaving the only people who really cared about her behind.

Mrs Goulding was still chatting to the cab driver at the end of the driveway as Bea slipped through the garden gate unseen. She headed down the mews behind the palatial Georgian townhouse. The beautifully appointed home where her sister had made a life for herself with Jack Wolfe—through hard work, honesty, integrity, courage, perseverance and an independent spirit Bea had always lacked.

She took off her heels and slipped on her sister's gym shoes and her sweatshirt over the revealing dress. It was only a couple of miles to the bank where she had an account containing the small inheritance her mother had left her, as well as a safety deposit box with the Irish passport she'd been able to apply for a year ago—thanks to an Irish grandfather—with some fanciful notion of one day using her language skills to start a new life in Europe. One of the many, many things she'd never had the courage to actually do.

The bank was open until noon on a Saturday.

She broke into a run, adrenaline helping to cover the fear clawing at her throat.

She wasn't brave or smart or determined like her sister. She had always been pathetic and insecure and indecisive. But if she was ever going to turn herself into someone she could be proud of, she had to begin somewhere. And hitting rock bottom for the second time in her life felt like the perfect place to start.

*Two days later*

'Mr Foxx, there's a Katherine Wolfe here to see you. She doesn't have an appointment but she's quite insistent.'

'Send her up. And hold my calls,' Mason said to the receptionist, then shoved his phone into his back pocket. He strode through the suite of rooms that he kept at his flagship hotel in Belgravia and used as a London base for his business.

He'd spent two days trying to track Beatrice Medford down after she'd run out of his loft. He would have preferred to hear from her, but her sister would have to do. For now.

The fury, though, which had been building all weekend, tightened its stranglehold on his throat. He forced himself to breathe through it.

*Don't let her see you give a damn. That's the only way to deal with these people.*

But what the hell was Beatrice playing at? And where had she gone? Because her father didn't even know.

The old bastard had shown up at the Foxx Grand in Belgravia on Sunday morning, after Mason had been forced to contact him in an attempt to locate his daughter. Medford had been all obsequious smiles and bonhomie, believing Mason and his daughter were now an item. It had taken Mason about ten seconds to realise Medford had no idea where she was. And once Mason had told him he hadn't seen her since Saturday morning, the old man's pale blue eyes had filled with irritation—but no sign of affection or concern.

It had given Mason pause.

But the moment of hesitation—about the way he'd spoken to her—was swiftly quashed.

She'd obviously gone off in a huff. Because Mason had figured out the truth. Perhaps she hadn't been home yet because she didn't want to break the bad news to her old man that there would be no marriage proposal from their latest billionaire mark—but there might be an unplanned pregnancy. Unfortunately, that didn't alter the fact she could even now be carrying his child, which meant he needed to find her. Pronto.

He paced in front of the lift, waiting for her sister to appear.

He was going to give Beatrice hell when he finally located her—for putting him in the untenable position of having to contact Jack Wolfe's wife to ask her where her sister was, like a lovesick fool. Instead of a man who lived up to his responsibilities.

He dismissed the memory of her face, the pale skin pallid with shock, her huge blue eyes sheened with distress while she shot out of his apartment as if her feet were on fire.

A memory which had resurfaced at regular intervals since Saturday morning. But which he refused to dwell on.

If she hadn't wanted him to call her out, she shouldn't have come on to him in the first place.

And made him think she had given him something precious, when her virginity had just been another bargaining tool.

The lift bell pinged, but as the doors slid open he found himself straightening, taken aback by the fierce look in Katherine Wolfe's eyes as she marched out.

'Mason Foxx, I presume,' she remarked with enough derision to be insulting. 'You bastard. Where is my sister?' she demanded, her glare hot enough to melt lead.

'I don't know,' he replied, raising his voice to match hers.

Unlike her father, though, who had been indifferent to his younger daughter's whereabouts, Katherine Wolfe looked ready to start ripping his place apart to find her sister.

'You must have some idea,' she countered. 'Because, other than my housekeeper, you appear to be the last person to have seen her. And if you don't want me calling the police in the next ten seconds...' she jerked her phone out of her purse 'and demanding they question you, you'd better tell me what you did to her on Friday night.'

'Are you nuts?' he shouted, the prickle of unease at the mention of the police only infuriating him more. Once upon a time he'd been terrified of the law. Scared the things he'd once had to do to survive might come back to destroy his new life... But not any more. 'If I knew where Beatrice was,' he added, 'why the hell would I have contacted you?'

'Oh, yes,' she sneered, stuffing her phone back into her purse. 'Your very cryptic message about needing to get in touch with her ASAP. Why do you need to get in touch with her?'

'That's between me and Beatrice and none of your business.'

'Well, I'm making it my business, Romeo. Did she spend Friday night with you?'

'Yes,' he said, damned if he would lie about that. He had nothing to be ashamed of.

'And then you just kicked her out the next morning after you slept with her, is that it?' Katherine Wolfe's glare narrowed. 'Of all the heartless...'

'I didn't kick her out. She left,' he said, beyond furious now. Who did this woman think she was? And what exactly was she accusing him of?

'But you must have said something, *done* something, to have upset her,' she demanded again.

'Why must I?' he replied, getting royally sick of the third degree. But, even so, a prickle of unease crawled up his back. The memory of Bea's devastated expression the next morning—and the feel of her body, relaxed and trusting against his when he'd woken up, coming back full force.

'Because my housekeeper said she arrived at our place on Saturday morning, bedraggled and distraught,' Katherine Wolfe replied. 'She left me a weirdly cryptic note that didn't make a lot of sense. And then she disappeared.'

'She…*what*?' he asked, his fury fading as another unwanted memory blindsided him. Of when he'd thrust heavily inside her, and she'd flinched.

He hadn't meant to hurt her. Hadn't known she was a virgin. Because she hadn't told him. But why hadn't she contacted him since that night? It had been over forty-eight hours and he hadn't been able to get in touch with her.

'She disappeared…' her sister said again, then gave a deep sigh.

Her shoulders wilted, the fierce expression fading. She paced to the large bay window which gilded the suite in spring sunshine. With her back to him, he could see the temper draining away, until all that was left was tension.

'Bea can be flaky at times, but one thing she would never do, unless she was having a major crisis, is cavort around London while not looking her best,' she said, her voice trembling slightly. 'Appearances are important to her because she hasn't got a lot else to bolster her self-esteem, thanks to our pig of a father.'

'What did you mean, she's disappeared?' he asked, his stomach twisting.

He hadn't *meant* to hurt her when they'd made love, that much was true, but he *had* meant to hurt her the next morning, and he was feeling less comfortable about that now.

Katherine Wolfe turned to face him.

'She's not at our father's place. And her phone has been switched off since Saturday night, because Jack pulled a few strings to get the mobile company to check it. I discovered this morning that she's emptied her savings account and the safe deposit box where she was keeping her ID documents. But I've contacted all her friends… or, rather, her acquaintances, as Bea doesn't really have any close friends…and no one's seen her.'

Katherine sighed, the vulnerability in her eyes reminding Mason of Beatrice for the first time.

The Medford sisters were nothing alike physically. Katherine was shorter, with an abundance of curves and a shock of in-your-face red hair—while Beatrice was slender and tall, her naturally blonde hair giving her a fragile grace. But as Katherine stared back at him, looking scared, he could see a definite resemblance…

Because, like Beatrice, when he had unloaded on her and she'd said nothing, Katherine had the same hopelessness in her eyes.

'I've been begging her to get away from our father for years, so maybe this is a good thing,' she murmured. 'Our father would have seen the press pictures from the Cascade launch, so he will have had expectations about your relationship. Expectations he would have tried to bully Beatrice into fulfilling for him, because that's the way he operates.' She tugged her bag strap in a nervous gesture as the last of her temper deflated. 'She definitely hasn't contacted you since she left you on Saturday?'

Mason's stomach churned. The picture Katherine Wolfe had just painted of Beatrice's dysfunctional relationship with her father was not the one he had assumed.

'No, she hasn't,' he murmured—which was the truth. But not the whole truth.

He had to find her and speak to her. To make sure she wasn't pregnant.

But he could see now that the reason she hadn't contacted him might be more complicated than he had assumed. Maybe she wasn't just sulking or trying to enhance her bargaining position.

Had he overreacted on Saturday morning because he'd always hated being taken for a mug?

It triggered stuff from way back. But had he let that baggage from his childhood cloud his judgement where she was concerned? Because he hadn't given her much of a chance to explain herself…

'I need to get back.' Katherine glanced at her phone. 'If she does contact you, would you let me know? Or, better still, get her to contact me. Or I'll worry.'

'Sure,' he said, although he knew Beatrice wasn't going to contact him.

'Look, I'm sorry I went off at you,' Katherine added, the easy and apparently genuine apology surprising him even more. 'But I've been frantic. I've always looked out for her. She's my baby sister.' She sighed heavily. 'But maybe it's time I let her stand on her own two feet.'

'Actually, there is something,' he said as she turned to leave.

'Which is?' Katherine asked, a flicker of impatience joining the concern. But for some reason it didn't annoy him as much now.

The two sisters obviously had a close relationship. The sort of relationship he had never experienced and didn't really understand. But which he could probably use. Because if Beatrice was going to contact anyone, it was likely to be this woman.

'She may be pregnant,' he said.

'She… *How*?' Katherine Wolfe replied, the searing look back with a vengeance. 'Do you mean to say you didn't use protection?'

'I used a condom,' he said before she could work her way back up to a full head of steam. 'It burst.' He decided not to mention that he hadn't checked the use-by date, because none of this was any of her business. 'I made an appointment for her with my doctor. If she is pregnant, I want to know about it.'

'Which is code for what, exactly?' Katherine's voice rose as she got way ahead of herself again. 'That you plan to make her have a termination?'

'Did I say that?' he snapped back, as the anger he'd managed to bank returned. He didn't explain or defend his actions or his choices to anyone, not any more. 'The point is, I have a pressing reason to find her too. So if *you* locate her, you need to let *me* know.'

Katherine's eyes narrowed, but then she swore—a word he wouldn't have expected to hear from the mouth of a member of the British aristocracy. But then Katherine Wolfe was turning out to be almost as much of a surprise as her sister.

'Fine.' She sighed again. '*If* Bea contacts me, I will tell her you wish to speak with her. But that's all I'm prepared to do. It appears my little sister has finally decided to start making her own decisions, and the least I can do is respect that,' she said, each word loaded with a thinly veiled warning. 'I think the least you owe her is to respect her choices too,' she added pointedly, before sweeping back into the lift and stabbing the button.

As the doors closed behind her, Mason tugged out his mobile and tapped out a text to his PA.

Hire the best private detective you can find. Cost not an issue. Beatrice Medford has done a runner and I need to locate her ASAP. NO STONE UNTURNED.

He pocketed the mobile as soon as he got Joe's thumbs-up emoji. But as he headed back into his office he knew he wasn't going to get any work done today as the vague feeling of unease intensified.

Yeah, he'd respect Beatrice's choices. But only if her choices didn't involve never contacting *him* again. He needed to know if she was pregnant. But, more than that, he realised now, he also wanted to know why she'd run.

# CHAPTER SIX

*One week later*

'*SIGNORINA*, YOU MUST be careful—do not get any more rides with strange men,' the kindly old farmer said in gruff Italian as Bea reached for the door handle of his truck.

Good advice from Signor Esposito, given what had happened with the last strange man she'd accepted a lift from, Bea thought wryly.

Then admonished herself for thinking about *him* again.

She pushed a weary smile to her lips as she shouldered her rucksack.

'Thank you, Signor Esposito, and don't worry, I will be very careful,' she replied in fluent Italian as she hopped out into the tourist bustle at the seafront in Rapallo.

The familiar pulse of panic was joined by a surge of loneliness as she watched him drive off. Signor Esposito had been a godsend, giving her a lift all the way to the Italian Riviera when he'd found her attempting to hitchhike for the first time in her life just outside Bobbio. His kindly, avuncular manner had made her feel safe after a terrifying few days. She'd never travelled alone before. And certainly not without considerable funds. It had been an eye-opener to discover how tough it was to get anywhere without the benefit of her father's money, a personal tour operator or a mobile phone because she'd had hers pinched in the Gare du Nord.

She hefted her pack onto her shoulders with a perkiness she didn't feel but was determined to fake.

*Buck up, Bea. Being on your own and incommunicado is a good thing. You need to learn independence and self-reliance.*

The last ten days had certainly been a baptism of fire—as she'd wound her way through France, into the Swiss Alps and eventually through the north of Italy—while becoming increasingly aware of her dwindling funds.

But her solo travels had taught her some valuable lessons already. Such as: you get a much better choice of hostel bed if you arrive early; long hair is a massive pain to wash in coach station toilets; two-euro sunblock does the same job as a two-hundred-euro designer brand; and only accept rides from men old enough to be your granddad.

She swiped her hair behind her ears, disconcerted by the savagely short cut which she still hadn't got used to after getting it hacked off by a Turkish barber in Bern. See lesson *numero due* in Bea Medford's Lessons Learned While Panic Backpacking Around Europe.

She took a moment to absorb the bustle of the port town on the Santa Liguria peninsula—and the beauty of her surroundings. Cafés and restaurants lined the road in between the palm trees, the tables already packed with tourists months before the start of the summer season.

She'd had no destination in mind when she'd left London on the Eurostar over a week ago—back when she'd thought she could afford to splash out on train tickets. She'd been desolate and despondent—courtesy of her one glorious night with Mason Foxx and the horrific morning after—and had boarded the first train out of the UK.

She'd only ended up in Rapallo because this had been Signor Esposito's destination when he'd offered her a lift. But as she made her way along the waterfront the rich scent of roasting garlic and seafood filled her senses and the sun warmed her skin. Lavish villa hotels and resorts dotted the hills above, contrasting with the haphazard terraces of pastel-coloured houses which lined the harbour. She stared enviously at the clear blue sea lapping against the array of fishing boats and luxury yachts docked in the bay.

Surely the Italian Riviera was as good a place as any to change her life.

Firstly, it was several hundred miles away—both figuratively and geographically—from her former life in London and *him*. And it was a tourist hotspot. She needed to find work—and quickly. A tall order for someone who had never had a proper job.

She had realised, while sitting wide awake during the twelve-hour coach ride from Bern to Milan, she didn't know how to *do* anything. Except speak five European languages, not all of them fluently. So a tourist resort ought to be the best place to begin looking. She hoped.

After plucking up her courage and pushing way outside her comfort zone to ask for work at each café on the seafront, she soon realised the stupidity of that assumption. Apparently, if you had no experience you were about as useful as an ex-London socialite with a backpack when it came to securing bar or restaurant work. But in the last café she tried, a young barista took pity on her and informed her the resort hotels around Portofino would be recruiting housekeeping staff for the summer.

She had no idea what 'housekeeping' entailed, but as she started the trek along the coastal path to Portofino, with her pack digging into her shoulders and the tiredness making her legs feel like overcooked spaghetti, she decided she had time to figure it out.

'You must change sheets, towels, yes?' Signora Bianchi, the housekeeping manager of the old-fashioned resort hotel tucked into the cliffs above Portofino, rattled off instructions in Italian as she led Bea into a palatial suite.

The view from the room's *terrazzo* was stunning, taking in the glint of a pool below and the stepped terraces leading down to a private beach and dock. Bea got precisely two seconds to admire it before she was led into the suite's bedroom.

'Vacuum and polish until everything shines,' the woman added, indicating the many marble surfaces and the worn carpet. 'Then you must clean the bathroom, top to bottom, and replenish all toiletries. You have experience, *sì*?'

'Oh, yes, absolutely,' Bea lied, having never scrubbed a toilet in her life. But this was her new life, she decided, a life she was in control of at last. And supporting herself, however she could, was the first step on the ladder to becoming the new woman she wanted to be. And no longer the sort of woman men like Mason Foxx despised.

*You're not doing this for him. You're doing this for yourself. Remember that.*

'The rate is eight euros an hour. Shifts start at six a.m., finish at three,' the housekeeping manager continued. Bea nodded again. The rate was below minimum wage because the job offered room and board in a shared dorm, but that would be a major boon to her budget. 'You will have to work on every weekend for the first two months. *Bene?*'

'*Sì, bene, molto bene,*' she said, maybe a little over-enthusiastically when the older woman sent her a curious frown.

The *signora*'s gaze glided over the cheap summer dress and sneakers Bea had purchased in a discount store just outside of Paris. 'We have uniforms—find one which fits in the storeroom, the cost will be taken out of your first pay packet.' She checked her watch, all business. 'Your probation lasts two weeks and can start now.'

'*Grazie,* Signora Bianchi. I won't disappoint you, I promise,' Bea said, determined to make it so as they made their way out of the suite and down the staff staircase. It would be hard work, harder than anything she'd ever done before, but a heady sense of anticipation took hold as she was shown her cart and took a quick shower before getting dressed in the hotel's tailored uniform.

She was feeling considerably less buoyant when she finished her first shift four hours later, and crashed onto her bunk in the staff quarters she would be sharing with six other women. Her knuckles were raw, her shoulders felt as if someone had been pummelling them with a hammer and her legs hurt, because kneeling on marble floors was hell on your knees. But as she lay, staring at the clean but worn mattress of the bunk above, a feeling of pride and validation blossomed. And the panic and devastation from that morning a week and a half ago, when Mason Foxx had looked right through her, finally began to ease.

She wasn't doing this to make Mason Foxx think she was worthy. Because she would never see him again.

No, she was doing this for herself. And for that girl who had always believed she couldn't be anything more than a decoration, a distraction, a vacuous, insubstantial, flaky airhead whose looks and appearance and ability to attract male attention were her only worth. Something her father had taught her but Mason had reinforced, because all he had ever seen—or ever *wanted* to see—was the illusion her father had created.

Ironically, she actually *had* been invisible today to the guests at the resort—as she'd wheeled the cumbersome cart in and out of the vacant bedrooms in her maid's uniform. But for every toilet she'd made shine, every room she'd tidied and polished, every bed she'd smoothed fresh sheets onto and tucked with the precision her fellow maid and new best friend Marta had taught her, her confidence in her previously undiscovered work ethic increased.

Today, she'd achieved something of real value for the first time in her life. A day's work for a day's pay.

It was a surprisingly good feeling—despite her complete and utter exhaustion.

She held her hands up, frowning as she examined the chipped nails and sore, reddened skin. That said, she was investing in a pair of heavy-duty rubber gloves with her very first pay package.

As she fell into sleep, her life seemed full of new possibilities. New horizons. New dreams. Which were a lot more prosaic than the ones she'd once had—of finding someone to love her and value her, the way her father never had. But so much more achievable. Because now all she had to do to make her dreams come true was learn how to scrub a toilet properly.

It wasn't until three weeks later that Bea discovered she hadn't made her last catastrophic error of judgement, not by a long shot, and that her new life was not destined to be anywhere near as simple as she had assumed.

And that Mason Foxx would always be a part of her life now… Whether she got up the guts to contact him again or not.

# CHAPTER SEVEN

*Four months later*

'SIGNOR FOXX, the Presidential Suite is being made ready by our new housekeeping manager. Do you wish to order food or…'

'I just want to crash,' Mason interrupted the Portofino resort manager's welcoming spiel. He was shattered after the flight from New York to Genoa and the drive along the coast—a journey he'd undertaken on the spur of the moment because the private eye Joe had hired five months ago had finally got a whiff of Beatrice Medford's whereabouts.

He probably should have rented a driver as well as the luxury convertible at Genova City airport, but he'd needed time to clear his head after the long flight. And the update from the PI.

Apparently, the man had managed to track Beatrice's movements as far as Rapallo ten days after Mason had last seen her—but then her trail had gone cold.

She was probably holed up at one of the luxury hotels in the region, because the Italian Riviera was just her style.

Off course, there was no guarantee she was still here. But Mason had been too wound up to wait any longer for more news, after having waited months already for this much, so he'd broken off delicate negotiations in Long Island to buy a chain of motels so he could fly all the way to Italy.

But as he'd driven along the coast, the picturesque coastline had done nothing to improve his mood.

How could the woman have disappeared so completely? And why had she? And how come he hadn't been able to look at another woman, let alone date one, since she'd walked out on him?

Because it had begun to feel that his determination to find her was about more than just the need to confirm she wasn't pregnant.

Not just every time he woke up, hard and ready for her, his heart beating ten to the dozen and his body yearning to touch her again. But every time the memory of her distraught face when she'd walked out on him crept into his consciousness—which had really started to annoy him.

He didn't agonise over his past behaviour, because dwelling on it only led to regrets and indecision and, worst of all, weakness. And, anyway, Beatrice was the one who had nixed her chance to explain herself with her little disappearing act.

But as he waved off the bellboy to tote his own bag, the niggling thought that his search for Beatrice had become an obsession persisted.

'Shall I instruct the housekeeper to finish the room later, *signor*?' the manager asked as he swung open the door to the Presidential Suite.

The sitting area was bright and airy and scrupulously clean, and the view across the bay impressive. But the suite's furniture was worn and fussy, its design features stuck firmly in the nineties. From what Mason had seen so far, the whole place could do with a refresh.

'Nah.' Mason dumped his bag on the couch in the main room. 'She can finish. But then I don't want to be disturbed,' he added, dismissing the guy.

He just wanted to be left alone now. Maybe once he'd had a refresh himself, he could figure out what the hell he had been thinking, flying to Italy to chase down a woman he hardly knew but remembered far too vividly.

He slipped off his shoes, then carried his bag to the bedroom and opened the doors to a *terrazzo* that looked onto the coast.

The sea air overlaid the scent of lavender polish and potpourri. The August sun peeped through the clouds, the weather fresher than usual for this time of year. He stood for a moment to take in the view. The cluster of brightly painted houses that overlooked the harbour were defiantly picturesque. Incongruous super-yachts dwarfed the tourist boats and a few fishing vessels which bobbed in the blue-green water. But while the old *castello* which had been converted into this hotel had an enviable position above the Ligurian Sea, he noticed the cracks in the plasterwork and the fading grandeur of the terrace below, where a smattering of tourists braved the sea breezes lounging beside an old-fashioned pool.

Definitely ripe for development, although business wasn't at the forefront of Mason's mind… Just like it hadn't been for five months, because he'd been distracted and out of sorts ever since that night in March.

That needed to stop now. Perhaps that was why he'd raced all the way here, not to chase the shadows from that night which had refused to die, but to finally put an end to this unhealthy, irrational obsession once and for all. Beatrice couldn't be pregnant, because she would have let him or her sister know, so she could hose him for support payments.

It was past time to let the fallout from that night, and her attempt to trick him into a commitment, go.

The sound of a toilet flushing dragged him out of his navel-gazing and an unseen woman's voice began humming a pop tune. The sweet, seductive melody floated into the bedroom from the en suite bathroom, making adrenaline spike in Mason's groin.

*Seductive?* What the...?

He tensed, shocked by his physical response, as the maid sang the words to the chorus in English. In an English accent.

Okay, he was officially losing his mind, because her voice sounded like...

Then the maid stepped out of the bathroom, her head bent, carrying a bucket and mop.

He couldn't see her face, only the short cap of blonde hair cropped close to her head. But the tailored lines of the hotel's blue uniform did nothing to disguise her slender figure, or her rounded belly as she turned to close the bathroom door.

The spike of adrenaline became a wave, slamming into Mason with devastating force. Why did the maid remind him so much of Beatrice?

When her hair was too short. And the society princess he'd met that night would never be seen dead working for a living. Perhaps because this woman's pregnant bump reminded him of the dreams which had tortured him, ever since that night, of his child growing inside her…

He thrust his fingers through his hair. Damn, was he actually losing his mind for real?

But then the vanilla scent hit him, and the wave of confusion turned into a blast of heat… Potent, provocative and devastatingly familiar.

'Beatrice?' he murmured, sure he had to be dreaming now or going mad.

The maid's head lifted. She dropped the bucket, splashing dirty water onto the carpet.

'Mason!' she whispered, looking almost as shocked as he felt.

Recognition slammed into him, and all but knocked him off his feet, as his gaze shot from her flushed, beautiful face—only made more striking by the boyish haircut—to land back on that tell-tale bump.

It *was* her. How was that even possible?

But then all he could seem to focus on was her belly. And his astonishment was overtaken by a visceral mix of anger and disbelief… And something that felt disturbingly like desire.

'Is that mine?' he ground out on a rusty gasp of fury.

* * *

*That?*

Indignation barrelled through Bea's body, overriding the cocktail of other emotions battering her—shock, panic, guilt, arousal—*arousal*, seriously?

Her hand cupped the place where her baby grew, instinctively protecting it from the emerald glare of the man not ten feet away from her—who she'd convinced herself she wouldn't have to see again, until she was ready.

'No, *that* isn't yours, it's mine,' she said, her voice surprisingly calm given she had just been dropped into a waking nightmare.

What was Mason Foxx doing in Portofino, in the Presidential Suite of her hotel? Was he the Very Important Guest her manager, Fabrizio, had told her about half an hour ago?

Or was his presence in front of her an apparition? A terrible manifestation of her guilty conscience, which she'd been studiously ignoring for months. For four months and twenty-one days, to be precise, ever since the lovely Dr Rossi had confirmed she was pregnant. Had this illusion been sent by the Do-the-Right-Thing Fairy to force her to stop avoiding the inevitable and contact the father of her child?

But the tall, broad-shouldered man in worn jeans and a T-shirt, his jaw covered in beard scruff, his dark chestnut hair finger-combed into waves, his eyes stark with shock and his tanned features flushed with outrage, looked far too real and solid and forbidding to be a figment of her guilty conscience.

The searing emerald gaze narrowed dangerously.

'Answer the question. Am I the father?' he said, throwing out a hand to indicate her belly but not shifting his gaze from hers—as if the evidence of her pregnancy was like Medusa, and if he looked at it directly he would turn to stone.

The indignation protecting Bea from her shock at seeing him again—alive and well and as much of a judgemental bastard as she remembered—was joined by a healthy dose of disgust.

A part of her wanted to lie, to tell him no, this baby wasn't his. Because he seemed less than pleased at the prospect. And her baby deserved the best of everything, including a father who wanted it to exist.

Discovering she was pregnant four and a half months ago had been an enormous shock, because she had totally convinced herself the early signs of her pregnancy were all phantom ones. That her tiredness, her one light period and her tender breasts were just a result of the shock to her once pampered system of having to get up before dawn and do manual labour for eight hours straight.

But the confirmation of her condition and the options available to her—delivered in Dr Rossi's measured voice—had also been a massive wake-up call. Because, as she'd come to terms with her new reality and realised she didn't want a termination, she had also realised that every single cowardly, self-serving, foolish, reckless, impulsive mistake she made from now on would have consequences. Not just for her, but also for her defenceless child.

She'd been determined, before that life-changing moment in Dr Rossi's office, to prove she could make a life for herself here. But discovering she was going to have a child had nearly broken her resolve. She'd been so close to calling her sister to beg for her help. She had even considered—in a particularly low moment during a gruelling shift cleaning up after a debauched party in the Honeymoon Suite while battling low-grade morning sickness—returning to her father's house in London. But somehow, she had powered through the panic and the anguish, and the physical exhaustion of early pregnancy, and come out the other side a better, more focused person.

She'd worked slavishly in the months since, enough to get a temporary promotion when Signora Bianchi had to take some time off, and she had even managed to move out of the bunk room into a place on the hotel grounds. She was no longer the society princess Mason Foxx had treated with such contempt. Nor was she the pathetic, easily cowed girl who had allowed herself to be bullied her whole life, and who had run away rather than stand up for herself.

She was a stronger, more determined person now. Maybe she still didn't have a long-term plan for her life—and her baby's life. And maybe she still struggled to deal with confrontations, which was why she hadn't contacted Mason months ago. But she had made the decision to have this baby. Alone. So she did not need him to be a part of its life.

So, while it would be wrong to lie to him about his part in making this child, she could give him a way out.

'You don't have to be the father,' she said, reasoning desperately. 'If you don't want to be.'

The frown on his face became furious. 'What the hell is that supposed to mean? Either I'm its…' He paused, looking unsure of himself for the first time since she'd met him. His Adam's apple bounced as he swallowed, as if he was struggling to even say the word *father*… 'Either I got you pregnant, or I didn't,' he continued. 'So, which is it?'

'If you're asking me if your sperm created *my* child,' she said, pressing her palm over her belly to protect her bump from that judgemental glare. 'Then yes, it did.'

He swore again, making her stiffen.

'But, as far as I'm concerned, that's where your involvement ends,' she added. But her voice was no longer steady, all her resolve and determination—and the courage she'd worked so hard to earn over the last five months—fading in the face of his fury.

'Like hell it does.' His gaze raked over her belly, then he scrubbed his hands down his face. 'There'll be a kid walking around in this world with my DNA. That makes me involved.' She noticed the tremor in his fingers before he jammed his hands into his pockets. Something about the evidence of his panic downgraded her own.

This man had treated her appallingly all those months ago. And she hadn't deserved it. He'd never given her a chance to defend herself. So what right did he have to behave like the injured party now?

'When were you planning to let me know you were having my kid?' he demanded, but she could hear the tremor in his voice too.

And suddenly she understood. He was trying to hide his fear behind a wall of outrage. She'd had months to get used to the news, he'd only had five minutes. While she didn't believe he was a good man, after the way he'd discarded her so callously, it occurred to her that he was probably in shock.

The knot in her belly loosened, and the weightless feeling of inadequacy—which had marred so much of her childhood and adolescence whenever she'd appeased her father—dissolved a little more.

'I don't know,' she said honestly. 'When I was ready to face your anger, I guess.'

His brows shot up his forehead and he swore again, but colour slashed across his cheeks before he marched through the terrace doors.

Was that shame she had seen in his face? Or was she projecting?

She followed him onto the *terrazzo*, surprised to find him sitting on one of the loungers, his forearms perched on his knees, his gaze fixed on the horizon. He didn't look angry any more, or even shocked. He looked shattered.

'I'm not angry.' His gaze met hers, then drifted down to focus on her bump. When his gaze returned to her face, she saw something in his eyes that shocked her even more than his surprise appearance at the Portofino Grande.

Uncertainty. Confusion. And awareness.

'I'm just…' He raked his hair back from his

face and stared out at the bay again, the blank stare making her sure he couldn't see the famous harbour, or the verdant coastline framing the sea. 'Hell, I don't even know what I'm feeling right now.'

She sat on the lounger opposite him, the spurt of sympathy surprising her. But she understood how scary it was not to be able to process your emotions—because she'd spent so much of her life unable to process her own. And she had the sneaking suspicion that Mason Foxx rarely even examined his emotions, let alone processed them. So there was that.

'I understand,' she said. 'I was shocked too when the doctor confirmed the test results.'

His head swung round, the accusatory stare destroying the brief truce. 'And when was that, exactly?'

Her pulse rate leapt and the tension in her stomach returned. She stood and brushed shaky palms down her uniform, determined to steady herself. She needed to fortify herself before she dealt with his anger—because she was probably in shock too.

Making this baby had been an accident, but it was one she was more than prepared to live with.

'Perhaps we could meet again later to discuss all this?' she offered, not prepared to be subjected to his inquisition before she'd had a chance to properly adjust to his presence in Portofino. She glanced at the water stain on the carpet where she'd dropped the bucket. 'I need to clean up the mess I made, and then finish my shift.'

But as she attempted to walk away, he leapt up and grabbed her wrist. 'Not so fast.'

The shock of his touch shot up her arm, before she could tug it loose. 'Please don't touch me.'

He frowned but released her. 'Okay.' He tucked his hand back into his pocket. 'But I want answers *now*. And I'm not prepared to wait.'

She scowled at him. 'Well, tough, because I have work to do.'

He let out a bitter chuckle. 'Is this some kind of a joke?' He flicked his finger to indicate her uniform. 'Since when do you work for a living?'

The muscles in her spine stiffened and it was her turn to glare.

He'd accused her of being a freeloader before, of having no pride or self-respect. And at the time he had been partly right. But he wasn't right any longer, and she refused to allow him, or anyone else, to belittle or denigrate what she did for a living, or what she had achieved in the past five months. Maybe being a chambermaid wasn't the pinnacle of human endeavour, and maybe her income was a minute fraction of his, but she had a prodigious work ethic now, and she happened to be exceptionally good at what she did.

'Since I decided to start supporting myself,' she replied as calmly as she could manage while her insides were tying themselves in knots. 'So I no longer had to be at the mercy of men like you.'

She walked back into the main living area and knelt down to clean the carpet with the stiff dignity of a queen.

The mocking sound was impossible to ignore when he followed her into the room, but she didn't look up. She needed to regroup, rethink, figure out what all of this meant. But one thing she refused to do was be judged or bullied by him again.

But then she heard him speaking into the house phone. 'Hi, send another maid up to clean the room.'

He'd slammed the phone back down before she could object.

'How… how dare you?' she spluttered, getting to her feet. 'I'm perfectly capable of finishing the job. Of all the high-handed, overbearing… You had no right to…'

'I have every right,' he interrupted her, slicing through her indignation with a nonchalance which was meant to enrage—and didn't fool her for a second, because his tanned skin was flushed with temper. 'I happen to be a paying guest. And I don't want you cleaning my damn carpet when I've spent thousands of pounds trying to locate you—not to mention torpedoing an important project in the Hamptons yesterday to catch the red-eye here—with the vague hope of finding you and talking to you.' His gaze skated over her belly again. 'And that's before we even get to the fact you're gonna have my kid, and you chose to hide out here playing chambermaid instead of telling me that.' His voice rose in anger. 'For five solid months.'

She flinched, then hated herself for the show of weakness.

She opened her mouth to shout back at him. But had to shut it abruptly when Marta appeared at the door to the suite, looking anxious and flustered.

'Signor Foxx, I am here to clean your room. Signor Romano wishes to know if there is a problem with Beatrice's work,' she said, sending Bea an apologetic look.

Marta knew what it was like to deal with difficult guests. And she had always covered for Bea, especially in the early days when her pregnancy had exhausted her far too easily. But Marta's 'don't worry, I've totally got your back here' look only made the tangle of nerves in Bea's belly tie themselves into a knot.

Marta couldn't help her with this situation.

'There's no problem with her work,' Mason barked in reply. 'But tell Romano he's giving Beatrice the rest of the day off.'

Marta coloured but managed to hide her surprise admirably. 'Yes, *signor*.'

He turned to Bea, who was momentarily speechless in the face of his arrogance.

'You've got half an hour to change and meet me by the red two-seater in the forecourt. Don't make me come and find you…again,' he added, before stalking into the bathroom and slamming the door.

Bea stood, shaking, her insides churning so hard now she couldn't think, let alone move. But worse was the creeping feeling of panic and inadequacy which she'd thought she'd tamed after five months of surviving on her own.

Marta's hand touched her shoulder. 'Who is this man? Are you scared of him?'

Bea shook her head. She wasn't scared of him. That much, at least, was true.

'Is he the father of the baby?' Marta asked, flooring Bea for a moment. How did her friend know? Was it that obvious?

But she found herself nodding again.

'And he did not know of its existence?' Marta added.

Again, Bea was forced to nod.

'So, this explains his temper, yes?'

'Tantrum, more like,' she murmured, but Marta's observation had forced her to face one uncomfortable fact. She really should have contacted Mason months ago.

'He is very rich and powerful according to Fabrizio,' Marta murmured, her lips quirking. 'And very hot. But if you do not wish to go with him, I will tell him you are sick. And cover for you with Fabrizio until he is gone.'

Bea blinked, then wanted to hug Marta for being such a loyal friend.

If only she could take her friend up on the generous offer to cover for her so she could flee. But where would she go? She had established a life here. And she had the baby to think about too. Also, with Mason in his current master of the universe mood, she would be putting Marta's job at risk as well as her own if the other maid tried to defy their Very Important Guest. And Marta didn't deserve to be put in the middle of her drama with Mason just because she'd had the bad judgement to befriend her.

Bea was forced to shake her head. 'It's okay.'

Mason was right about one thing, at least. They did need to talk.

Strictly speaking, this was a conversation she should have had the guts to have months ago. And avoiding it any longer would not make it any easier.

'*Grazie*, Marta.' She gave her friend a hug of thanks. 'I need to go with him and get this over with…' Although she had the feeling that this conversation was unlikely to be the end of anything. 'But if you could keep the fact I'm spending the afternoon with Mr Foxx quiet, I'd appreciate it.'

The hotel had a rule about fraternising with guests. But somehow the thought of breaking it felt like the least of her worries. That said, it was just more proof of how little consideration Mason had given to her situation by basically ordering her to spend the afternoon with him.

But, frankly, what did she expect from a man who wore his arrogance like a badge of honour and clearly still thought she was beneath his contempt?

Marta nodded, but then her lips quirked. 'Make sure you wear your best dress.' She glanced at the bathroom door, behind which they could hear the shower running. 'A man like this deserves to be kept waiting. So he will know—just because you are a maid you are no pushover.'

Beatrice nodded. But as she took the back

stairs she had the awful feeling that Marta was wrong. Bea the pushover was still lurking inside her, just waiting to reappear in a crisis.

A good forty minutes later, Bea headed back through the hotel grounds to the forecourt. After considerable debate, she had donned a light summer dress with sunflowers on it, which was too tight around her breasts and the bump, but otherwise flattered her figure.

Mason's tall frame dwarfed the expensive sports car as he leant against it. He'd folded his arms over his broad chest in an impatient stance which highlighted the tattoo circling his biceps. His eyes were shaded by a pair of aviator sunglasses which had probably cost more than her monthly salary—but she could still feel his scowl.

'You're late,' he remarked.

She dug her teeth into her tongue to control the knee-jerk apology for her tardiness which almost popped out of her mouth. Mason sneered at politeness, she already knew that. And, anyway, she didn't have anything to apologise for—give or take the odd secret pregnancy.

'I don't take orders from you,' she replied, pleased when he stiffened and drew himself up to his full height.

If he thought he could still intimidate her,

she would be sunk. So she would just have to fake a confidence she didn't feel. Until she did feel it. *Easy.*

His brows flattened. But as he yanked open the passenger door she could see she'd surprised him with her ballsy response. Good.

*Welcome back, Bea the badass.*

'Get in,' he said.

She glared at him for two long seconds to make it clear she would get into the car when she was good and ready, then folded herself into the passenger seat.

He slammed the door with enough force to make the car shake.

*Strike two to Bea the badass.*

For once, she didn't care about inciting a man's temper. The thought was surprisingly liberating as she watched him climb into the driver's seat without a word, the dark frown radiating his disapproval.

Unfortunately, as the car fishtailed out of the hotel forecourt, spraying gravel onto the lawn, and he accelerated down the short driveway and onto the coast road, her newfound confidence disappeared into the rear-view mirror as she was forced to grab the expensive leather seat in a death grip.

# CHAPTER EIGHT

'PLEASE SLOW DOWN.'

Mason glanced at his passenger, but before he could tell her he didn't take orders from her either, his gaze snagged on her belly. And his pulse rate shot straight back into the danger zone.

She seemed calm, her short hair plastered to her head and accentuating that stunning bone structure, the simple cotton dress flattened against her breasts. Why did they seem fuller than when he'd last seen her? Was that a result of her pregnancy too? Just one of the changes to her body caused by his child?

*His child.*

He swallowed convulsively, surprised by the urge to ask her about every detail of the pregnancy.

Then he noticed her fingers white-knuckling on the car's upholstery.

He eased his foot off the gas to take the next

bend, as the car wound its way along the coastal road back towards Rapallo.

Killing them both—and the bump—was not going to improve this situation.

Or lower his heartrate.

Or help him to think coherently. His mind had gone AWOL ever since he'd spotted her in the hotel room in that maid's outfit.

But that was no excuse to behave like an idiot.

He shifted into first to take the fork in the road, which led to an exclusive cliff-top restaurant at the top of the peninsula. He'd located the Michelin-starred *trattoria* on his phone while he'd been waiting for her, then offered them a small fortune to secure a table, cancel all their other bookings for the rest of the afternoon and compensate their guests.

He considered it money well spent. Because he didn't trust himself to be alone with her while they had this discussion, but nor did he want an audience of tourists taking snaps of them together and posting it on social media.

And, frankly, twenty grand was a drop in the ocean compared to what he'd already shelled out on the private investigator to facilitate this conversation.

They arrived at the restaurant, perched on the brow of the hill, with only one table set on the terrace which looked out over the point.

The maître d' rushed out to greet them. 'Signor Foxx, we are delighted to welcome you to Del Mare,' he said, bowing as he opened Beatrice's door. 'I am Giovanni. All is prepared as you requested.'

'*Grazie*,' Mason murmured as he climbed out of the car and threw the keys to the parking attendant.

But as he placed his palm on the small of Beatrice's back to escort her into the restaurant behind Giovanni, she stiffened and stepped away from him.

'I can't… I can't eat here, Mason,' she whispered, a stubborn frown on her face.

'What's the problem?' His gaze flicked to her belly. 'Is it the seafood?' he asked, as it occurred to him that he knew absolutely nothing about what pregnant women could and could not eat.

Her eyes widened, and then she let out a nervous laugh—which didn't exactly make him feel any better about all the stuff he did not know about her condition.

'No… It's not… I'm fine with seafood. It's just…' She glanced at the maître d', who was waiting a respectful distance away. Then she leaned closer, giving him a lungful of that intoxicating vanilla scent. 'I can't afford to eat here.'

He stared at her for a moment. Was she joking? But she didn't look as if she were joking, from the embarrassed flush on her cheeks.

'I'm paying,' he said flatly.

'But I don't want you to pay,' she insisted. 'I'd like to go Dutch.' She held out her hands to encompass the exclusive restaurant, the terrace framed by wisteria vines which afforded them a breathtaking view of the coastline. Silver cutlery and crystal stemware sparkled in the sunlight on the solitary table set especially for them. 'But this is way outside my budget,' she added. 'Could we please find somewhere a bit cheaper? I know a great pizza place in Rapallo that does lunch for under ten euros.'

It was his turn to frown. She *was* actually serious.

For a moment, he was lost for words.

What had happened to the society princess, the Medford Ice Queen, a woman used to living in the lap of luxury and expecting other people to pay for it? Because this was not the woman he had slept with all those months ago.

Or at least, not the woman he had assumed he'd been sleeping with.

Of course, maybe he should have expected this. After all, he had just found her scrubbing toilets for a living in a second-rate hotel.

He'd convinced himself while waiting in the car park that her menial job had to be a trick to garner his sympathy. But he was starting to doubt that conclusion. Exactly how long had she been working at the Portofino Grande? Because, according to Romano, she was the housekeeping manager, and as far as he knew she'd had no experience with any kind of work when they'd met five months ago.

But then his surprise turned to irritation.

If she'd needed cash, she'd had another good reason to contact him. And yet she hadn't.

Her new financial independence wasn't the only big change, though. She'd held her own when he'd freaked out in the suite. She hadn't cried or wilted or cowered or sulked, the way he would have expected. She'd stood up for herself. He'd seen glimpses of that woman five months ago, but apparently Beatrice Medford was now a fully-fledged Valkyrie.

A part of him—a *large* part of him—didn't like this new, improved Beatrice—because getting her to do what he wanted was going to be tougher. But another part of him had a grudging respect for what she had achieved.

And seeing her spirited response to him had been a major turn-on too. *Go figure.*

Of course, it was beyond stupid for her to have holed herself up here, trying to earn a living in a minimum-wage job when he was more than capable of supporting her—and he certainly intended to tell her that. But while he'd already decided she couldn't work at the Grande any longer, he couldn't quite bring himself to demand she do as he said.

He'd crushed her spirit once before. And he was beginning to realise he didn't feel nearly as justified about doing that as he once had.

Of course, changing restaurants was non-negotiable, but perhaps he could figure out a way to get her to agree to eat here without stomping all over her pride.

'I don't want to eat somewhere too public, Beatrice,' he explained. 'If the press get hold of photos of us together, we're going to have a problem on our hands…'

*On top of the massive one we've already got—that you chose to hide out in Portofino instead of letting me know I was your baby daddy.*

She blinked as if the thought had never occurred to her, as he tried to cut off his resentment while another thought reverberated in his head.

*Did she ever intend to tell me about the pregnancy?*

'Don't you think you're being a little paranoid?' she said, but the stubborn tilt of her chin had softened. 'I doubt there are any British tabloid journalists hanging out at Pizzeria di Rapallo. And I'm not news any more. The

Medford Ice Queen is dead and gone. And good riddance.'

The comeback surprised him, but not as much as the vehemence with which she announced the demise of the woman she had once been. Or, rather, the woman the press and her father had pretended she was. Not for the first time, he wondered how he had never thought to question that image.

'You're noticeably pregnant,' he said, still trying to be persuasive, even though this discussion was getting them nowhere. 'And if any photos end up on social media of the two of us having a heart-to-heart, precisely five and a half months after the last time we were splashed all over the internet together, it won't take long for the press to figure out whose baby it is,' he continued.

The bitterness stuck in his throat again.

Why *hadn't* she told him? Did she think he wasn't good enough to be her baby's father? Was that it?

'We've got this place to ourselves for the rest of the afternoon,' he added. 'So we can discuss this without an audience.'

'How did you manage that?' she asked, her eyes widening as she set off on another pointless tangent. 'This restaurant is always booked out months in advance.'

'I wanted privacy for this conversation,' he

said, his frustration and impatience torpedoing his desire to be reasonable. Time to cut to the chase. 'And I was prepared to pay for it. If you want to go Dutch on the cost, you can take out a loan another time. But right now we're wasting time and money. And I'm beginning to think this is just another of your tactics to avoid telling me why you decided scrubbing toilets in Portofino made more sense than letting me know I was going to become a father.'

She stiffened, but he could see the flicker of guilt in her eyes.

*Bingo.* Maybe she genuinely wanted to pay her way, but she was also not keen on having this conversation.

*Well, tough.*

'That's not true,' she said at last, but the tremble in her voice told a different story.

'Then prove it and stop arguing about nothing. I've been trying to find you for five months, Beatrice. And I'm entitled to know why you didn't contact me as soon as you knew about junior,' he said, forcing himself to look directly at her bump. Which, thankfully, was now only hitting a solid seven on the freak-out scale.

He could see she still wanted to argue, but as she gripped the strap on her purse, her head swinging between him and the maître d', he could also see her indecision. Because Beatrice was nothing if not completely transparent. Thank God that was one thing about her which hadn't changed.

Her gaze finally met his, and she sighed. 'Okay, fine. But if we ever share a meal again, I'm paying.'

'Agreed,' he snapped, then cupped her elbow and led her into the restaurant.

As they followed Giovanni to their table he noticed how the pulse on the inside of her arm battered his thumb. And how her vanilla scent added a rich sultry note to the refreshing aroma of summer blooms and sea air.

She swept her hands over her bottom to sit down, and a rush of blood hit his groin.

There was no *if* about it. They *would* be sharing a meal again, because one thing was for damn sure—he had no intention of letting her out of his sight any time soon.

Bea listened to the waiter reel off a list of special dishes, grateful for the interruption. She sat ramrod-straight and stared at the horizon, unnerved by the luxury of the deserted restaurant, which felt like revisiting another life—and the intense scrutiny of the man opposite her. She could *feel* his gaze on her and sense his forceful presence across the table. Which was unnervingly reminiscent of their one night together.

His attention had been so exhilarating then, and it still had the power to make her skin prickle and her heartbeat throb low in her abdomen even now.

If only she could read him as easily as he seemed to be able to read her.

She knew he was furious with her for not contacting him about the baby. She also understood that reaction and had been ready to confront it. But somehow his silent assessment now made her more uneasy than his temper had earlier.

She picked up the menu—to stop her hands trembling—and made herself glance his way.

Just as she had suspected, he was watching her, but his fierce expression was more thoughtful than hostile.

She let go of the breath clogging her lungs. It would be better if this didn't have to be a confrontation.

She was glad she'd spoken up about his choice of restaurant, though, even if he had steamrollered over her objections. Because she had sensed a willingness to negotiate which hadn't been there when he'd demanded she go to lunch with him.

*Progress?* Of a sort.

The waiter stopped talking and she picked the only entrée she could remember from the list. Mason ordered the same.

The waiter took the menus and left. But as

Bea went to place her now unoccupied hands in her lap, Mason leaned across the table and snagged her wrist.

His touch, as always, was electric, and she couldn't control the instinctive shudder as he opened her fist and ran his thumb across the calluses on her palm.

She tugged her hand free, feeling stupidly embarrassed when she had nothing to be embarrassed about. She worked for a living now. Why should she be ashamed of that?

'How long have you been working as a maid?' he demanded.

Her cheeks heated. 'I'm not housekeeping staff any more. I'm the housekeeping manager.'

His lips quirked, the half-smile making the muscles in her spine stiffen. Maybe she'd overestimated his newfound respect for her.

'Okay, how long have you been the housekeeping manager?'

'Not long, only since Signora Bianchi had to take leave when her husband had a stroke,' she said. 'I stepped up because Marta didn't want the extra responsibility,' she added, eager to fill the charged silence, and give him more of an insight into who she was now. 'Marta has two young children and Fabrizio was only offering an additional five euro an hour to take the position for the rest of the summer.' She barrelled on. 'It means having to organise the rotas, ensure all the rooms are ready each day before three and train new staff,' she continued. 'Plus, I have to ensure the cleaning supplies are always sufficiently stocked and arrange the laundry...'

He held up his hand and she hesitated, ready for him to say something contemptuous or dismissive, but instead he murmured, 'You sound like you know a lot about the job.'

'I... I do. I like it,' she offered, surprising herself with the admission.

Over the past five months she'd learned so much—how to ensure the marble didn't streak when you rinsed it, how to fold the bed sheets until they bounced, and all the other cleaning hacks which earned her good tips and made sure her rooms were scrupulously clean and delivered on time. A lot of the work was drudgery and not something most former society princesses would aspire to, but she was immensely proud of the temporary promotion. She liked the greater responsibility. And the extra money had also been very welcome. She lived frugally, but it was difficult to keep within her means and she needed to save more for when the baby arrived—because she hadn't worked long enough in Italy to qualify for more than the most basic maternity benefits.

'Really?' His scarred eyebrow lifted. 'You actually enjoy cleaning up other people's mess?'

And there it was, the contempt she had been expecting. It upset her to realise it hurt more than it should. His opinion of her didn't matter. It never had.

'I was talking about the promotion,' she shot back. 'But actually, no, I'm not ashamed of cleaning. It's a job. And it means I'm not dependent on anyone any more.'

He gave a slight nod, his gaze narrowing as if he were seeing something he had never noticed before.

Pride swelled in her chest.

Even though his approval didn't matter, it felt important he see how much she had changed from that clueless, eager-to-please girl who had thrown herself at him. And convinced herself that losing her virginity to a man like him would somehow validate her as a woman. When she was the only person who could do that.

'I get it,' he said eventually, tapping his fingers on the table. 'Is that why you chose to hide out here and you didn't tell me about the pregnancy? Because you wanted to prove you could survive on your own?'

His tone was surprisingly non-confrontational, coaxing even, but she could hear what he hadn't said—that he thought she had been playing at being independent just to annoy him.

She took a deep breath, eased it out slowly to keep her temper in check.

The waiter appeared with a bottle of sparkling water, some freshly baked focaccia and a saucer of olive oil to dip it in, giving her a chance to gather her thoughts.

She had prepared a hundred persuasive answers to the question of why she hadn't contacted him sooner over the last five months, but she could see now, every one of them had been riddled with half-truths and blatant lies, as well as assumptions about how he would respond to the news of her pregnancy, which she didn't know him well enough to make.

He'd been incredibly cruel to her that morning—not just in the judgements he'd made about her, but the way he'd spoken to her... But the night before, he had been very different, treating her with care and tenderness, while taking responsibility for the burst condom. She still didn't know which of those men was the real Mason Foxx—the arrogant, overbearing bastard who had accused her of terrible things or the man who had held her in his arms and shown her a pleasure she had never even believed existed.

She eased another steadying breath out through tight lungs, attempting to quell the burst of awareness. She needed to focus, because his nearness had always had the potential to derail her common sense.

She dropped her head, stared at the hands clasped tightly in her lap. She examined the reddened skin on her knuckles, the small burn on her thumb from when she'd ironed her uniform for the first time—and gulped down the shame which threatened to gag her.

'I guess that's part of it,' she admitted, forcing herself to meet that probing gaze.

The truth was, she *should* have contacted him as soon as she'd known she was pregnant. And he deserved an honest answer. Or as much of an honest answer as she was capable of giving him.

'You… You accused me of things which weren't true. I hadn't intentionally seduced you to get a marriage proposal out of you for my father's benefit,' she managed, hating the defensiveness in her voice and the way his eyes sharpened.

Did he still think her virginity had been a trick to snare him? Why should she care if he did? What he'd said had been ugly and hurtful, but by protesting her innocence was she giving him permission to make those accusations in the first place?

But he didn't say anything, didn't challenge her, so she forced herself to continue and say what needed to be said.

'But you *were* one of several men on a list my

father had given me that afternoon.' She gulped down the ball of humiliation in her throat, sickened again by how easily she had once allowed herself to be manipulated. And how little she had done to fight against—or even call out—her father's cynical agenda. 'He told me he wanted me to…' she lifted her fingers to do air quotes '…*engage with* you. That's why he hired a stylist and an expensive designer gown and a chauffeur-driven car to take me to the event. So you were right about his intentions. But when I met you, I didn't know who you were, and when you told me your name…' The heat seared her collarbone, but she made herself continue. 'I already felt…*something*… With you. And it had nothing to do with his list or fulfilling his agenda.'

'Something, huh?' One dark brow lifted, the scepticism in his expression not letting her off the hook for a second. 'I think you're going to have to do better than that, Beatrice.'

Bother. Apparently, he was not going to be satisfied with euphemisms. But then why would she have assumed he would be? Mason Foxx was nothing if not direct. It was one of the things she had once found so attractive about him.

She cleared her throat.

Why was it so hard to talk about that livewire connection, when they'd made a baby together? It was just sex after all, and chemistry. It had only been a big deal for her because it had been her first time, her *only* time. But the emotional connection she had kidded herself they'd shared that night had all been in her head.

'Well, you were very hot, and I responded to you in a way I hadn't thought I'd ever respond to anyone...' She hesitated to take a gulp of the fizzy water. 'Sexually speaking,' she continued, impossibly grateful suddenly that he'd probably paid a king's ransom to empty the restaurant. 'My father created the Medford Ice Queen to snare men like you and Jack Wolfe.' She stared at her hands again. 'And, although I had been unhappy for a long time, and had even taken language lessons with the vague idea of coming to Europe and breaking away from his influence, I had let him believe I was willing to be that person. And I'd never explicitly disabused him of that fact.'

She raised her head to find him watching her, but the accusation had gone, to be replaced by a disturbing heat she recognised.

She looked away again, across the cliffs, determined to ignore it. Surely this continued attraction was nothing more than an inconvenient leftover from the physical sensations she had never been able to forget from that night?

*Don't fall into the trap of mixing insane chemistry with intimacy and affection again—because that will only make you vulnerable.*

Maybe Mason Foxx wasn't as unreasonable or unstable as her father, but he was still a powerful man who didn't do soft or tender. Having a relationship with a man like him would always have been a disaster.

She met his gaze. 'I didn't really have a plan when I left London,' she continued because he hadn't said anything, his reaction impossible to decipher. 'I just knew I needed to change. *Everything*. I ended up in Rapallo by accident. And the job at the Grande was pretty much the only one I could get without any experience. But after a while, things just started to fit.'

The waiter reappeared, accompanied by a female assistant holding a tray aloft. After laying two plates on the table, he whipped off the silver covers to reveal heaped helpings of the seafood linguini they'd ordered.

Her stomach knotted with apprehension. The scent of garlic, roast tomatoes and chargrilled langoustine filled Bea's senses. But she'd never felt less like eating anything in her entire life.

As the waiting staff left, Mason picked up his fork and began twirling the pasta. As he swallowed the first bite, still not responding, she felt irritation collide with the bundle of nerves in her stomach.

She coughed, loudly.

He glanced up from shovelling the pasta into

his mouth, swallowed. 'Why aren't you eating?' he asked.

*Seriously?*

'Because I'm not hungry. I can't eat. Until I know what you have to say.'

'About what?'

She threw her hands up, exasperated. 'About everything, Mason. About becoming a father. About finding me again. About what I just told you… Stuff like that!' she huffed, so frustrated now she could scream.

Was he playing some kind of game with her? Trying to unnerve and antagonise her?

But when he placed his fork back on his plate, his demeanour didn't appear manipulative or confrontational. Good to know she could read that much at least.

'The way I see it…' The tight muscle in his jaw started to twitch, but she had the strangest feeling his fury wasn't directed at her any more. 'Your father is a bully, who doesn't give a damn about you, except what he can get out of you. He showed up at my office the day after you disappeared, and straight away I recognised the type. Because my old man was the exact same, just without the peerage and the posh accent and the expensive suits. A sewer rat willing to sell his own kid to the highest bidder. I don't blame you for wanting to escape from that.' The barely leashed aggression shocked her a little, but not as much as the pulse of compassion at the glimpse into his childhood.

It was all part of the Mason Foxx myth, that he'd had a rough start in life. But the details had always been deliberately vague, steeped in rags-to-riches romanticism to make the Foxx Group's CEO seem invincible while also being a brilliant brand ambassador for aspirational luxury.

But as he ran his thumb over the scar on his brow, and she glimpsed the barbed wire tattoo on his collarbone which had fascinated her that night—and fascinated her still—she wondered about the reality of his rough start. What price had he paid to become a success? What experiences had given him the drive and ambition to escape? And had he really been able to leave that boy behind? Because beneath the anger and bitterness directed at the father who had exploited him, she also detected an odd note of regret, even guilt, which didn't fit at all with the myth he had created for himself.

'I'm glad you broke free of that bastard,' Mason continued, dropping his hand from his face as if he had just noticed the habitual gesture. 'I also owe you an apology for the way I reacted that morning. Which I can see now had as much to do with baggage from my childhood as it did with finding out about your old man's agenda.'

'What baggage?' she asked, astonished not just by his forthright apology, but also the way it made her feel—both vindicated and seen.

'Just…stuff.' He shrugged, clearly unwilling to elaborate.

Had he said more about his past than he'd intended?

She quashed the foolish burst of compassion and hope. She'd allowed herself to get emotionally invested before, when she was lying in his arms that night, kidding herself the physical intimacy they'd shared had meant something more. She couldn't make that mistake again. Because there was so much more at stake now. Not just for her, but also her baby.

*Their* baby.

She let the thought sink in. It had been so easy not to engage with Mason's place in her child's life while she was working her backside off to create a new life for herself. It was a lot less easy while he was sitting across from her, his broad shoulders stretching his T-shirt and his stubbled jaw reminding her of the feel of his lips on her…

She pushed down the unwanted blast of heat.

*Focus, Bea, for Pete's sake.*

'It's not important,' he said evasively, the intense gaze becoming hooded. 'The point is,' he continued, lifting his fork again, to wind it into the pasta, 'I guess I can understand why you ran off, but that doesn't explain why you didn't tell me that…' He ducked his head to indicate her belly. 'That our night had consequences.'

*That? It? Junior? Your condition? The pregnancy? Consequences?*

Was it significant that whenever he referred to their baby, he used impersonal terms? He'd made a massive deal about the fact she hadn't informed him of the pregnancy, but at the same time he hadn't given her any hints about what he felt about becoming a father.

'I intended to tell you, eventually,' she said, determined to believe that was true. She'd come so far. Enough to know she wasn't a coward any more. But contacting him had seemed overwhelming.

'I guess I kept putting it off to focus on other things… Like making a living,' she added, which was mostly true. 'And because I was scared about how you would react to the news.' Which was absolutely true. Her emotions whenever she thought about telling Mason had swung violently between panic and fear and guilt, so it had been simpler not to think about telling him at all. 'So I took the easiest option and just kept putting it off. And for that *I* owe *you* an apology,' she said, finally getting to the point.

Whatever his views on fatherhood, she hadn't had the right to keep this pregnancy a secret.

She'd made the decision to have this baby—*their* baby—without involving him, and she refused to regret it because she still didn't know how he would have reacted if she'd told him straight away. But it didn't matter what he might have said and done then, because it was academic now.

His brow furrowed with disapproval. But instead of berating her again for failing to contact him sooner, he shoved the pasta into his mouth. He chewed and swallowed, then gave her a stiff nod.

'Okay. Apology accepted,' he said, his tone tight, and a little grudging, but his gaze direct. 'I guess we both made mistakes.'

Relief washed through her. The knots in her stomach loosened.

Maybe this didn't have to be as hard as she had thought it would be.

But then he shot a pointed glance at her untouched food. 'Eat up before it gets cold. Then we need to discuss next steps.'

*Next steps?* What *next steps?*

Was he going to make demands and ultimatums? To dictate what would happen now? Because she was not about to compromise the independence she'd worked so hard for to kowtow to a man—even the scorching-hot billionaire who was the father of her child…

*Scorching-hot? Where did that come from? So not the point, Bea.*

Her skin flushed as she lifted her fork and concentrated on her food to beat back the latest wave of anxiety.

Mason Foxx was still a virtual stranger. She needed to get to know him better before she made any more assumptions about him. Good or bad.

They'd both apologised for past hurts, the wrongs they'd done each other. She had no idea what he could possibly mean by 'next steps'. But the fact it sounded so ominous could have more to do with her own insecurities, and the huge power imbalance between them, and that heat which would not die, than any malign intent on his part.

She still didn't even know what he felt about the pregnancy—other than angry she hadn't told him sooner. So it made sense to nurture this tentative truce.

And to avoid getting hung up on his scorching hotness! *Sheesh.*

Unfortunately, as they ate in silence—him demolishing the tasty pasta dish, while she picked at hers—the knot in her stomach and the hot brick in her abdomen refused to get the memo.

# CHAPTER NINE

*'YOU WERE VERY HOT, and I responded to you in a way I hadn't thought I'd ever respond to anyone... Sexually speaking.'*

Mason polished off the last of the seafood linguini, his voracious appetite for food covering his voracious appetite for something else entirely—as the words Beatrice had murmured about their night five months ago spooled through his head on a loop. And forced him to acknowledge something he'd been refusing to engage with for five solid months.

He still wanted her. *A lot.*

Their unfinished business wasn't just sexual any more, might not *ever* have been just sexual—but sex was the one thing he felt comfortable focusing on. Her confirmation that her reasons for choosing him to take her virginity had never had anything to do with her father only made him eager to focus on it more.

Because that volatile sexual chemistry—

which he had felt the first moment he had laid eyes on her—hadn't dimmed in the slightest.

It also explained a lot of things which had been confusing him for five months. Why he hadn't been able to forget her. Why he'd spent a fortune tracking her down. Why he'd dropped everything and flown out to the Italian Riviera. Where the weird kick of joy as well as shock had come from when he'd spotted her in the maid's uniform and discovered she was pregnant with his baby.

On some basic, elemental level he just wanted her to be his.

He didn't believe in fate, or kismet, or love at first sight, or any of that other romantic stuff people used to justify their basic instincts. But he did believe in biology and chemistry. Which had to be why he had staked a claim to Beatrice that night, which couldn't now be broken.

The baby was an abstract concept to him in a lot of ways. He had never thought of becoming a father, probably would have laughed in the face of anyone who had suggested he would ever *want* to get a woman accidentally pregnant. But with Beatrice, he couldn't suppress the thought that their current situation didn't feel like a trap so much as an inevitability.

An inevitability he could use.

He had no idea how long the need, the yearning, the urge to possess her and protect her would last. After all, he'd never felt this way about anyone before—as if he had a sexual connection with them that was so strong and real and intense it might actually go beyond the physical. But one thing was certain—after five months of being desperate to find her, he planned to explore it.

As he watched her pick at her food, though, he could sense her nerves.

However hard she had worked to reinvent herself, one thing remained the same—she was still vulnerable. Much more vulnerable than she probably realised.

She had been blindsided by their intense physical connection that night too. Which was even less of a surprise. She had been a virgin, plus she had spent her life up to that point being bullied and coerced by her father. He hadn't lied when he'd told her he knew what that felt like. How it could destroy your self-esteem. Although he wished he hadn't revealed quite so much.

Thank God he had managed to stop himself blurting out the truth about his mum too.

She didn't need to know about the things he'd done to survive, to escape. Because then she might start questioning whether she wanted him within fifty feet of this baby.

*Their* baby.

He swallowed the last bite of pasta as the waiter arrived, disturbed to realise that Beatrice's reaction to his past might matter to him. He'd always been determined to curate his own story, but now, more than ever, he was glad he'd kept the sordid details of his past out of the public eye.

He certainly did not want her to know that his mum had abandoned him—or she might wonder why she had. Which was something he'd asked himself a thousand times over the years… And the only answer that made sense was that there was something in him his mother had been unable to love.

He didn't need Beatrice's love, but he was beginning to realise he wanted a commitment from her. So, letting her know that even his own mum hadn't wanted to stick around was not a smart move.

'*Il dolci*, Signor Foxx?' the maître d' asked.

'No desserts, thanks, Giovanni, we're finished here,' he announced. 'Charge my credit card and add a five-hundred-euro tip and, thanks, it was delicious.'

Giovanni beamed, then whisked the plates away. As the man disappeared, Mason dropped his napkin on the table and stood.

'But Mason, we… We haven't discussed next

steps yet?' Beatrice's face was a mask of confusion, but he could see her apprehension too.

He was glad she was off-kilter, because that could work in his favour. But he also needed to get her to relax enough to be amenable to what he had to say.

He knew how to negotiate, but he was used to negotiating from a position of power. And he didn't have all the power here. Thanks to his irrational behaviour five months ago, and his freak-out an hour ago. Plus, he'd never wanted anything as much as he wanted Beatrice Medford back in his bed.

The pregnancy could be a boon or a bust in that respect, he wasn't really sure which. And her newfound independence was another obstacle which could go either way. She couldn't really enjoy scrubbing toilets for a living but, at the same time, he could see that earning her own wage—after spending so long under her father's thumb—had to be seductive.

And the truth was, even their sexual connection wasn't necessarily going to work in his favour, as Beatrice seemed oblivious to exactly how powerful and rare it was.

'Let's head back to the Grande to have that discussion,' he said.

Until he figured out how to deal with all the

variables, he wasn't about to play his hand. Which meant stalling. For now.

Her eyes widened. 'I… I don't think that's a good idea. If Signor Romano sees me going to your suite, he'll want to know why.'

He frowned. He didn't give a damn about Romano. As far as he was concerned, her job was over now anyway. She couldn't keep working as a maid—he drew in a breath—or even a housekeeping manager. Not now he'd found her.

But he forced himself not to lose his cool. Because it would be totally counter-productive when it came to Operation Get Beatrice to Relax.

'Then let's head back to your place. Where do you live?' he asked, suddenly realising he was curious.

She frowned. She wasn't too keen on that idea. But he could also see she didn't want to risk breaking their truce. 'I live on the grounds of the hotel. I guess we might be able to sneak to my trailer without being seen.'

*A trailer?* She was living in a mobile home… What the actual…?

He bit his tongue, schooled his features. 'Terrific,' he said. 'Let's go.'

But as they made their way back to the car, he could feel his hackles rising again. What had she been thinking?

As he drove down the coast road at a more sedate pace, he promised to do whatever it took to make Beatrice see sense.

Because no way in hell was he going to allow the mother of his child to live in squalor, doing manual labour for pennies, hundreds of miles away from where he could keep an eye on her.

'Watch your step, it's rocky here,' Bea said, aware of Mason's pricey high-tops as he followed her through the grove of gnarled lemon trees.

He hadn't said much on the drive back, but she had sensed his disapproval when she'd directed him to the unpaved road which led to the overgrown terraces banked into the cliffs above the hotel. But her heart lifted as they came out of the old orchard and approached the mobile home Marta and her husband had helped her to tow up here a month ago.

With rent in this area way out of her price range, she'd spent the last of her inheritance buying the third-hand mobile home after spotting it in a car park in Rapallo. She'd negotiated with Fabrizio to let her park it on the unused land, hooked up the electricity and water supply to the kitchen below and spent all her spare time cleaning, repairing and decorating it. She had a spectacular view from the porch she'd constructed from old crates and planted with flowers and herbs in a cluster of pots. Stringing solar-powered fairy lights through the branches of the surrounding lemon trees had turned her new home into an enchanted citrus-scented oasis—and she loved sitting here in the evenings, doing translation work for the nearby tourist bureau to supplement her income.

Space was at a premium inside the trailer, with a tiny box shower and composting toilet, a compact lounge/kitchenette and a bedroom at the back taken up entirely by her one extravagance—a queen-sized bed—but she had everything she needed.

This was *her* place. She no longer had to share the bunk room with the seasonal staff.

She fished the key out from under a pot of fresh basil and opened the door, aware of Mason's silence.

She hadn't wanted to bring him here. The man was a billionaire who had walk-in wardrobes bigger than the home she was so proud of. But as she entered the neat, scrupulously clean and well-ordered kitchen and lounge area, she refused to let it bother her.

'Would you like a cup of tea?' she asked from behind the counter.

'Sure,' he said without enthusiasm.

He had to duck to get in the door. And with

his head skimming the low ceiling, his presence instantly made her home look more cramped than compact.

'How long have you lived here?' he asked, his gaze gliding over the bright, colourful furnishings which she had borrowed or sourced at local markets and thrift stores—and convinced herself were vintage and eclectic.

'Just over a month,' she said, busying herself with the tea-making. 'I love it. It gives me privacy and freedom, and it's affordable. Signor Romano takes a peppercorn rent and the utility fees off my wages and the evenings are stunning here, with the scent of bougainvillea and lemons in the air and the heart-stopping view across the bay towards Portofino.'

'Uh-huh,' he said with a distinct lack of enthusiasm as he settled on the two-seater couch which made up her living area. The old frame creaked under his weight, and when he stretched out his long legs, his feet almost touched the opposite wall.

She waited for the water to boil, aware of the huge chasm which existed between their lives. But she couldn't resist the opportunity to watch him, unobserved. His shoulders were impossibly wide as they stretched across the back of the couch. His hair was shorter than it had been that night, when she'd fisted her fingers into the silky waves and held onto him as he sank into her.

And made a baby.

She blinked and concentrated on the tea, the flush of heat so intense it was uncomfortable. And embarrassing. But as she poured the boiled water into her teapot and arranged a tray with two mugs and some freshly baked amaretto cookies, the hot brick in her abdomen continued to pulse. How come she could smell him over the almond scent of the amaretti and the citrus from the trees outside? That intoxicating aroma of woodsy cologne and laundry detergent and sandalwood soap which had her remembering far too forcefully the feel of him, making her his.

*Not his, Bea. You belong to no one now but yourself and your baby.*

But then she frowned at the tea tray. She added a bowl of sugar and a jug of milk—and tried to contain the foolish wave of emotion at the thought that she had made a baby with this man but she had no clue how he liked his tea.

*Which is why you allowed him to come here. Because you need to know him better.*

Heat scorched her cheeks.

*Just not in the biblical sense, even if your sex-starved body is comprehensively contradicting you on that score.*

Which had to be the pregnancy hormones. Totally.

She started to lift the tray.

'Wait, I'll get that,' he said, and rose so swiftly from the couch the trailer rocked.

Then he was next to her in the tiny kitchen, his strong body close enough to touch. And smell not just the delicious woodsy cologne and the soap, but also the tantalising aroma of salt and man she remembered from that night.

He went to lift the tray just as she tried to step aside, and their bodies collided. Her breath caught in her lungs, her gaze trapped in his, her whole body alive with sensations she'd tried to forget. But hadn't. Awareness and passion darkened his eyes to a mossy green, and made her insides clench.

She couldn't seem to move. Almost as if in slow motion, he raised his hand and brushed his thumb down the side of her face. She shivered, her tongue darting out to moisten her lips, her throat so dry she felt as if she were attempting to swallow a boulder.

'I still want you, Beatrice,' he murmured, his rough voice barely audible above the blood rushing in her ears. 'I never stopped wanting you.'

His hand slid down to cup the back of her neck. She should say something. *Anything.* But she couldn't find the words to protest as his head bent to hers, his breath feathering across her lips.

'If you don't want this too, you have to tell me now,' he murmured.

But instead of calling a halt to this madness, her sob of surrender sounded like a gunshot in the cramped space.

His lips captured hers—claiming, branding—and his fingers threaded into her hair to cradle her head and anchor her mouth for his possession. The hot rock in her stomach plunged between her thighs and throbbed, the hunger and heat so familiar and yet different.

More demanding, more intense, so much more overwhelming.

Their tongues tangled, the dance of seduction both fierce and forthright and unstoppable, the heady haze of need descending so fast she couldn't think. All she could do was feel.

She kissed him back with a fervour she couldn't control. She grabbed his T-shirt to drag him nearer, until her bottom hit the counter and his lean abs pressed against the tight mound of her belly.

Hard hands grasped her waist and lifted her onto the counter, until she was perched on the edge, her legs splayed around his hips.

They broke apart. She needed air, she needed

time to think. What was she doing? Giving in to this insane desire was not smart.

But then he pressed marauding lips to her neck, forcing her head back against the cupboards, and palmed her breast.

Sensation spiralled down to her core with devastating purpose, and a moan escaped as he eased the front of her dress down, releasing one engorged nipple.

His lips captured the yearning peak, which was so much more sensitive now. She clasped his head to her chest, urging him on, as his palms trailed up her thighs, pushing her dress to her waist.

He swore softly and released her nipple from the delicious torment. The breeze from the open door made her aware of her bared breast, the nipple damp from his kisses, drawing tight. But then he shifted back, and her gaze locked on the thick ridge in his jeans.

Their eyes met, the flush of arousal slashing across his cheeks like the fire burning across her collarbone.

'Is this okay?' he asked, his hand hovering on the buttons of his jeans.

The harsh demand registered, but she couldn't seem to process what he was saying through the heady fog of desire.

'Will it harm the baby?' he asked again, as

he stroked the thick length, desperation turning his gaze to a rich emerald.

All she could do was shake her head dumbly, while her every thought was obliterated by the throbbing need to feel him inside her again.

He grunted, then dragged her panties down her legs, before finding the swollen nub of her clitoris with his thumb. She braced her hands on the counter, dropped her head back and gave herself over to his sure, devastating touch as he worked her into a frenzy.

She was panting, sobbing, as she flew to her peak, but just as the pleasure broke over her, she heard him fumbling with his jeans and releasing the thick erection.

Hooking her legs over his hips, he dragged her forward and entered her to the hilt.

She clung to his shoulders as his forehead touched hers, his harsh breathing matching her own. He gave her time to adjust to the overwhelming pleasure, the exquisite sensation, the intense connection. Then he began to move, drawing out, thrusting back, slowly, carefully but with a purpose, a determination which sent her careering back to that terrifying peak. The pleasure rose to crest again—so fast, too furious—the sensations consuming her vicious and unstoppable now.

The molten pleasure exploded along her

nerve-endings as she let out a feral cry of completion, shattering one last time. She heard him shout out, and fly over right behind her.

*What the hell did I do?*

Mason clasped Beatrice's bare hips and pressed his face into her fragrant hair, trying desperately to level himself. To take stock. To think past the bone-melting climax which had left him weak and shaky and strung out.

But he couldn't seem to battle his way out of the thick fog of afterglow. Couldn't seem to feel anything but the tight clasp of her body, massaging him through the last of his orgasm, and her hands, limp and trembling, as she clung to him. And couldn't hear anything but the thunder of his own heartbeat and the ragged pants of her breathing.

He'd just taken her like an insane person.

One minute they'd been standing too close in the cramped space, and the next he'd been dragging off her panties and thrusting heavily into that tight, wet heat.

His chest heaved as enough of his faculties returned to dump him off the glittering cloud and plunge him into brutal reality.

He shifted back, felt her twitch as he moved away from her.

She looked shell-shocked, dazed, her breathing uneven, her nipple reddened where he had mauled it moments ago. He braced against the swift spike of desire as she banded an arm across her chest to cover her nakedness.

Shame engulfed him as he stuffed himself back into his jeans.

He bent to pick up her underwear, brutally aware of her struggling to repair her own clothing. He clasped her elbow to help her get down from the narrow counter. As she landed on her feet, she tugged her arm free, and shame closed his throat.

What could he say to make amends? He'd planned to be smart, sophisticated, pragmatic, to reason with her about her living conditions, to persuade her to give up her job and let him support her... And then, eventually, to show her that whatever they'd shared in London wasn't over.

But, instead of that, he'd jumped her as soon as he'd scented her arousal and got close enough to touch.

He handed her the scrap of lace.

She grabbed it and slipped her panties back on.

'Thank you,' she said, the polite reply incongruous.

'I didn't use a condom,' he murmured. 'I'm sorry.'

Her gaze finally connected with his, but the vivid blush on her cheeks only made her seem more innocent. More vulnerable. And made him feel like more of an animal.

Where had all his cool points gone? Before Beatrice he'd always strived to be, if not charming, at least generous with women in bed. He knew he was rough around the edges, but he never wanted any women to be able to say he wasn't aware of their pleasure too. But with Beatrice, sex had always been different. It had never been fun, or light, or recreational. It had always been basic and elemental—a force of nature he couldn't control. He'd come close to losing it completely just now, and it shocked him.

'It's okay,' she said, running her fingers through her short cap of curls and breaking eye contact. 'Luckily, I don't think you can get me pregnant twice,' she added with a dry wit which might have been funny—if he hadn't felt so raw and exposed.

The comment brought the baby back to the forefront of his mind, the way it hadn't been as soon as she'd given him the go-ahead earlier.

The shame kicked up another notch.

She went to step around him, and he laid a hand on her waist to hold her in place.

'I haven't slept with anyone else since that night,' he said. 'And I've never taken a woman without protection before now,' he added, not even sure why he felt compelled to defend himself.

But when her eyes widened at his admission, the look in them doubtful, he knew why.

He'd accused her of using him that night, but the truth was, it had always been the other way around. He'd used *her*. Because she'd responded to him with an innocent enthusiasm which had made him feel connected to her in a way he'd never felt connected to any other woman. But he needed to be able to control it or he was in danger of becoming that feral kid again, looking for validation where there was none.

'Okay,' she said, sounding wary now.

He blocked her path as she tried to step around him again. 'Are you okay?'

Her brow furrowed, as if the question puzzled her. He'd bet he was the only bloke she'd ever slept with. He couldn't imagine her sleeping with other men when she was pregnant with his child, and all he'd shown her so far was hunger, and heat. The urge to show her tenderness, though, only confused him more.

'I had several orgasms,' she said, her cheeks flaming but her gaze unflinching. 'If that's what you're asking.'

He cleared his throat, the husky confession doing things to his self-control he didn't need.

'Actually, it's not.' He cradled her cheek, slid his thumb over the abraded skin he'd kissed too enthusiastically. 'The baby?' he managed. 'Will it be okay? I didn't mean to be so rough.'

She shifted away from him. And he was forced to release her.

He needed to get a grip and ignore the scent of sex filling the tiny kitchenette—not to mention the remnants of that mind-blowing orgasm still echoing in his groin—which were doing weird things to his libido.

'The baby's fine, Mason. You weren't that rough. I enjoyed it. I guess there was still some pent-up…stuff between us. But I…' She ran her hand down her face, clearly flustered. Why did he find that arousing too? 'I definitely don't think we should do it again,' she added. 'Because that will just complicate things.'

Everything inside him rejected the statement.

'Beatrice, they're already complicated,' he said, because there wasn't much point in avoiding the obvious. 'You're going to have a baby, which means you can't stay here doing this job. You do realise that?' he added, because he might as well get it out there. He had planned to be subtle, coaxing, persuasive, but he'd already torpedoed that approach.

He'd seen the way she'd beamed with pride when she'd walked into this broken-down trailer. And heard the sense of achievement in her voice when she'd talked about her job at the resort. But she needed to see sense now.

'Not when it's my child you're having,' he added. 'I won't allow it.'

He knew he'd made a major tactical error the minute he'd said it when she sucked in a sharp breath. He blamed it on the fact that all his brain cells had just been incinerated.

'That's outrageous, Mason,' she announced, her expression going from flustered to horrified in a heartbeat. 'You don't get to decide what I'm allowed to do just because I'm pregnant.'

*When it's my kid, yes, I damn well do.*

It was what he wanted to say, but he managed to hold onto the knee-jerk counter-attack as a few of his brain cells worked their way back out of his boxers.

The truth was, he wasn't entirely sure where the fierce desire to protect her and his child came from. Perhaps it was wrapped up in the shock of finding her pregnant—after having dreamed about it so often. Maybe it was the far too revealing revelations they'd shared at lunch, or the explosion of endorphins which he was still trying to get a handle on… But understanding his fierce need to stake a claim on this woman and ignoring it were not the same thing.

He couldn't ignore it, not any more. He'd tried

for the last five months and all it had done was leave him on edge—which had to explain why he'd gone off like a powder keg as soon as he'd been alone with her in a confined space.

'That came out wrong,' he said, trying for conciliatory now his cognitive function wasn't a total bombsite.

'Yes, it flipping well did,' Beatrice concurred, looking appalled.

'I just meant… I want you to come back to London. With me. I can buy you a place.' He let his gaze glide over the home she was so proud of, but which would never be good enough—for her or his baby. 'Which would be much more suitable than this one. And I want you to have the best healthcare.' Plus, she would finally be where he needed her to be, for his sanity, if nothing else. 'I screwed up with the condom, so you and the baby are my responsibility.'

'That's ridiculous, Mason. No, we're not,' she said, but she sounded more exasperated now than appalled—which felt like progress.

He'd made a total balls-up of this conversation in every possible way. But something about her expression made him glad he'd finally broached the subject of her returning to London. He'd never been a sophisticated guy—especially with her—so subtle would always have been a stretch.

'I chose to have this baby, not you,' she continued. 'I had options when the doctor confirmed I was pregnant, but I didn't take them.'

He sighed, but the tension in his ribs released as it occurred to him he was glad she hadn't.

'And I'm really not ready to uproot my life again,' she added. But when she chewed on her bottom lip in that distracting way she had, two things occurred to him. Not all her cognitive abilities were fully functioning yet either. And she was more anxious and less sure than she seemed.

Both things he could take advantage of, once he'd worked out a coherent strategy. But to do that he needed time to get his brain function fully operational again.

'Why don't we take a rain check on this discussion?' He cupped her chin and planted a kiss on her lips, satisfied when her mouth softened instinctively. 'I need to grab a shower first,' he continued, suddenly feeling lighter than he had in a while. Five months, to be precise. 'And so do you,' he added, sniffing the air, which was still heavy with the scent of sex. 'Or that smell is liable to turn me on so much I may have to christen the bed in this place too.'

'Mason, what the …? That's *not* funny,' she cried, sounding outraged as she slapped his hand away.

But he could see the stunned arousal turning the pale blue of her irises to black. And he knew she was no more immune to the scent of him on her skin than he was.

'We can go to the pizza place you mentioned in Rapallo,' he said, his regenerating brain cells starting to work overtime. 'And you can pay. What's it called?'

'Pizzeria di Rapallo,' she said, drawing out the words to emphasise her uncertainty. 'We can go for dinner and discuss this more. But I'm not giving up my life here, Mason,' she added. 'Or coming back to London with you. I can't. And I don't want to.'

*Yeah, you can, and you will.*

Because he was going to do everything in his power to convince her.

'I'll pick you up at seven,' he said as he backed out of the trailer, leaving her standing in the doorway looking deliciously rumpled and delightfully confused.

As he headed back to his car through the citrus grove, he dug his phone out and fired off a text to Joe.

Found B Medford in Portofino. Pregnant. Baby mine. @ Pizzeria di Rapallo tonight. Tip off press.

That took care of the stick.

He hated the tabloid press but she had to realise that, sooner or later, they would find her here, and when they did her life would be untenable. He was just speeding up the inevitable.

Now, all he had to do was come up with a persuasive carrot.

She'd mentioned studying languages, and he'd heard her speaking fluent Italian, making him wonder if she were a polymath. Plus, she knew more about the sharp end of hospitality now than most of his executives. Finding her a position in London that would satisfy her desire for independence and utilise her skills, while also giving her a much better salary and career prospects, would make it even harder for her to resist the inevitable.

He dismissed the tiny ripple of guilt as he shoved the phone back into his pocket. He had always been ruthless. It was a skill he'd developed to get over his mother's desertion and escape his father's failures without a scratch.

He frowned, climbing into the car. Or at least not any emotional ones.

Of course, that was also why he was unlikely to be a good father in the traditional sense.

But his ruthlessness was how he'd built a billion-pound legacy which his child and Beatrice could benefit from—even if he wasn't cut out to become a permanent part of their lives.

He began to whistle as he reversed the car

down the rutted track, feeling sure of himself again for the first time in five months.

The residual hum of desire pulsed in his lap as he remembered their frantic lovemaking in her trailer.

The fringe benefits of having Beatrice exactly where he wanted her, preferably somewhere less cramped and a lot closer to home, would be a perk they could both enjoy. Until their volatile sexual chemistry had worn off—which would, no doubt, be some time before she gave birth to his child. But when that time came, he planned to have fulfilled all his responsibilities to her and the baby—which would at least make him a better parent than the two useless people who had given birth to him.

# CHAPTER TEN

THE FOLLOWING MORNING, Bea woke feeling tired and unsettled, and still tender from yesterday afternoon's jump-fest in her kitchen—which had made sleeping all but impossible.

Every time she closed her eyes she could see Mason's face again, his eyes glittering with arousal and purpose, and feel him thrusting heavily inside her—taking her to places she had only ever been with him.

Her heart bobbed in her chest. And the familiar desire surged again.

She glanced at her alarm clock and groaned, then threw back the sheet. She had half an hour before her shift started.

But as she dragged herself out of bed she recalled their dinner date over pizza at the bustling eatery on the seafront, the tables packed as the sun edged towards the sea on the horizon—and her frustration increased.

Their conversation in Rapallo had been a lot less productive than their lunch date.

Because Mason had resolutely refused to listen to her. She didn't want to leave Portofino just because he felt responsible for their baby, or so they could have lots more great sex, or so he could offer her an amazing job—after questioning her extensively about her language skills... Because, as annoyingly tempting as all those offers were, she knew they were just bribes to bend her to his will.

It had taken her a while to get her heartbeat under control when he'd turned up at seven to collect her. And it had become harder and harder to say no. Because being in his company had brought back all those unwanted urges. *Again.*

It was lowering to realise that, despite a five-month separation, and the person she had become in that time, this man still had a powerful hold over her.

She should not have had sex with him. And not just any sex, but frantic, no-holds-barred, mind-blowing orgasmic sex. But during their meal she had managed to forgive herself for jumping him.

Mason Foxx was charismatic, edgy, ruggedly handsome, phenomenally successful and stunningly hot. Why wouldn't he make her weak at the knees? Even Marta had noticed his charms and she'd been happily married for five years and had two children under four. Plus, Mason was the father of her baby. Maybe it wasn't just her weak impulse control where he was concerned which was to blame, but also the biological imperative of seeking out the one person who could help protect her child?

Maybe that also explained the clenching sensation in her ribs when he had told her he wanted her to come back to London.

After taking a quick shower and donning her hotel uniform, she headed into the kitchen and began making herself her morning coffee— while resolutely trying not to relive yesterday's jump-fest again.

She really hadn't expected him to want to support her. The most she had hoped for was that he wouldn't hate her, for taking the choice away from him to become a father. But when he had laid out his plan, determined to give her and their baby whatever they needed to thrive, she had felt her wayward emotions getting the better of her again.

Which had made her even more wary of accepting his offer.

She didn't want to risk falling into her old habit of subjugating her needs to someone else's wishes. And she couldn't give up her independence. Not for anything. Or anyone.

The one thing Mason hadn't said, the one thing he had refused to be drawn on even, was whether or not he wanted to be an active part of this baby's life after it was born.

She frowned, her thoughts scattering as she noticed the ripples forming in her coffee. A strange rumbling developed. The sound became deafening, the vibrations so violent it made the cupboards rattle and the whole trailer shake.

She rushed to the door of the trailer.

Was this an earthquake? Did they have earthquakes on the Italian Riviera?

She flung the door wide, in time to see an enormous black shape darken the sky above, then glide over her head and drop down towards the terrace below.

*What on earth...?*

Then she noticed the Foxx Group logo emblazoned on the machine's side as it landed on the hotel lawn.

She was still staring at the helicopter when Mason marched through the citrus orchard, with an intent look on his face. Her heartbeat shot straight to warp speed, because she remembered that look from yesterday afternoon, when they'd made love in the trailer... And yesterday evening, when he'd walked her back here in the twilight, and she had resisted the powerful urge to ask him in for a nightcap—because she had known exactly where that would lead.

'You need to pack. We have to leave,' he said without preamble as he reached her.

'Why?' she asked, startled not just by the urgency in his voice but the desire to obey him without question—which could not be good.

'The press is here,' he said.

She heard it then, the commotion below them—a cacophony of shouts and pops no longer masked by the chopper's engines.

'Pictures of us together at the pizzeria last night are all over the internet,' he continued. 'Romano and the staff are having to hold them off until the security guards I've hired arrive.'

Shock came first, swiftly followed by guilt. He'd warned her this might happen when she'd first suggested eating at the pizzeria in Rapallo. Why hadn't she listened to him?

'I can't believe they still care,' she said inanely, struggling to adjust to the situation— and the wrenching realisation that her choices had just narrowed considerably.

She would have to leave. The Grande's clientele came here looking for a peaceful vacation, not to be besieged by paparazzi and journalists. Plus, she had just made Marta and Fabrizio and everyone else's jobs impossible.

'Of course they care,' he said, sounding surprisingly magnanimous, given the untenable situation she had created for everyone.

He had been right. Hiding out in Portofino indefinitely and pretending her past didn't exist had never been a viable option for the long term.

'Society Princess runs off to Italy to become a maid and have a billionaire's kid alone and in secret,' Mason added. 'It makes a great story.'

A story which he would be the villain of, she realised, as the last of her delusions about her situation came crashing down.

Why had she never considered how her choices would reflect on him? And the reputation he'd worked so hard to build. He'd said nothing last night about the negative press her situation would attract. But she should have realised how it would look if the press ever discovered she was living in Italy, doing a menial job while pregnant with his child.

'I've spoken to Romano,' he said, gently herding her back into the trailer. 'And your friend Marta. He's going to write you a final cheque and she'll meet us by the bird to say goodbye.'

She blinked furiously, devastated—at having to leave her life here so abruptly—but also stupidly touched that he had arranged everything so quickly.

She hadn't wanted to accept his help before. Had been determined to resent the loss of independence that would represent. But perhaps she should have realised she had already lost that by choosing to have his child.

She'd proved something incredibly important to herself during the last five months. That she wasn't useless, or pathetic, that she could thrive and prosper if she worked hard and showed initiative. But she had to face the reality now—of her situation, but also of his.

'But we need to go now,' he added, crowding her trailer again with his presence.

'Okay,' she said.

His eyebrows flew up. 'Really? No more arguments?'

'No, I understand,' she said.

All he'd wanted was to do the right thing. For her and their baby. And she needed to let him.

As she set off to pack up as much of her life in Italy as she could carry, it occurred to her that her confidence in her own abilities had never depended on where she was, or what she did for a living. Or even who she was with—even if that person was as overwhelming as Mason. All it had ever depended on was her own courage and determination.

As she said a hasty goodbye to Marta and Fabrizio and the other hotel staff by the Foxx Group helicopter—while the press shouted intrusive questions from the hotel car park, threatening to break the barricade being manned by Mason's security guards—a pang of regret and sadness pierced her chest.

She had found a home in Portofino. But she needed to move on and build a home for her baby as well now, which ought to include its father…

She settled into the helicopter as Mason spoke to the pilot. But as she strapped herself into the seat, instead of feeling compromised, or wary, her heart did a giddy two-step.

She didn't know if they could make this relationship work. She wasn't even sure they would still want to by the time the baby was born. There were so many things about Mason she didn't know, she frowned, including how he took his tea. But trusting to luck and her own judgement didn't seem anywhere near as scary as it had when she'd arrived in Rapallo five months ago.

She caressed her bump, remembering the explosion of hormones which had occurred in her trailer yesterday… The pulse in her abdomen became wild and insistent as Mason strode out of the cockpit, then folded his muscular body into the seat next to her.

'All good?' he asked as the helicopter's blades whirred above their head.

She nodded. 'Yes. And thank you.'

'What for?' he asked.

She smiled, enjoying his puzzled frown. For such a forceful guy, he wasn't always as sure about everything as he seemed.

'For rescuing me,' she said, nodding towards the press hordes still trying to clamber over the barricades. 'From that.'

His gaze intensified, then dropped warily to where her hand rested on her belly. 'Having got you into this mess,' he said, 'it was the least I could do.'

She wondered what mess he was talking about.

Then realised that might be why he hadn't wanted to talk about fatherhood. Because he simply didn't know yet how he felt about it.

But then the rest of his reply registered. And it occurred to her that other men would have done a lot less.

Why did it matter if he was unsure about his role in this baby's life? They had four months to figure it out now. Together.

Mason wasn't a bad man. And the desire between them was still as vibrant and exciting as ever. So why shouldn't they explore that too?

Her heart lifted in her chest as the big bird rose off the ground and the noise from the blades drowned out further conversation.

The smile on her lips sank into her heart as

the sun shimmered over the deep blue of the sea below, dazzling her… She and Mason and their baby *might* have a bright future ahead of them—as a family—something she'd always yearned for, but never thought she truly deserved… Until now. But how would she ever know if she didn't make the most of this chance to find out?

She waved goodbye to the first real friends she'd ever had, before the lush beauty of the Italian Riviera—where she had finally discovered the real Bea Medford—disappeared under the clouds.

But her heart continued to float on the flight to Genoa, and the journey on the Foxx company jet back to the UK—lightened by hope and determination and the promise of all the possibilities ahead of her, which she couldn't wait to explore.

# CHAPTER ELEVEN

THE SCENIC LIFT travelled up the outside of the Foxx Suites building—Tower Bridge looking suitably imposing as it spanned the river—while Bea grappled with the realisation that she had basically come full circle in five months.

She'd built her life back up from that low point—built it back better and stronger. She wasn't that panicked girl any more, but it still felt strange, and emotionally a little overwhelming, to be back at Mason's London penthouse again.

'Hey, you okay?' Mason asked, his hand stroking her back.

She glanced over her shoulder and sent him a tired smile. He'd asked that question constantly since the helicopter had left Portofino. And he couldn't seem to stop touching her, which—while kicking off those unruly desires—had also felt protective and comforting, sort of.

'Yes, it just feels weird. Being back here again. When I feel like a different person.'

He tugged her gently into his arms until her belly rested against his waist. 'I guess you're two different people now,' he joked.

She chuckled, grateful that he could joke about the baby. 'Yes, I suppose we are.'

As they walked into the lobby area he dumped the rucksack she had stuffed with all her most precious possessions several hours ago on the breakfast bar. Still a little dusty from her journey through Europe to get to Portofino and made of cheap nylon, her pack looked out of place on the sleek marble surface.

But then she felt totally out of place in the stunning designer bachelor pad.

She gulped down the tickle of anxiety in her throat.

Mason strolled to the kitchen area and poured her a glass of chilled water from the gleaming double wide refrigerator. She chugged it down gratefully. The throb in her abdomen returned when he tucked a short curl of hair behind her ear, the look in his eyes a mixture of bossy, possessive and intense.

Which was also super-hot. *Damn him.*

'If there's anything you need, just text,' he said, while she continued to drink the cold water. 'I can get the rest of your stuff in Portofino shipped over. I've had all my things cleared out, so the place is all yours.'

'You won't be sleeping here too?' she asked.

His lips quirked and she realised how needy she sounded.

But she'd assumed—had hoped, in fact—that they would be living together. She wanted to get to know him. Not just how he felt about the baby, about them, but everything, because he fascinated her—on so many different levels.

'Not sleeping, no,' he answered, the sensual smile suggesting he was enjoying her discomfort. 'I prefer my own space. But I'm hoping that won't preclude us sharing the bed here on a regular basis.' His gaze heated, and hot blood charged into her cheeks, while turning the throb in her belly into a definite hum. 'Or the kitchen counter. Lady's choice.'

'I see,' she said, or rather croaked, her throat having dried to parchment. She took another gulp of the icy water.

She could tell him she didn't want to continue their sexual relationship. But that ship had already sailed and hit an enormous iceberg on her kitchen counter in Portofino. Plus, the hum was making it clear a sexless relationship wasn't what she wanted.

But his decision to live elsewhere was more

problematic. How could she get to know him if he was hardly ever here?

'Why do you need your own space?' she asked, because it occurred to her that could be even more of an issue when the baby was born. Not that she expected him to live with them, exactly, if he wasn't comfortable with that. But perhaps it was time to start asking more direct questions about how he envisioned his place in this child's life.

He shrugged. 'I guess I've never been good at sharing,' he said cryptically. 'Plus, I'm a workaholic. I do a lot of travelling. I sleep, at most, five hours a night. And I've never had to tell anyone where I am or what I'm doing. Joe, my PA, knows my schedule. But that's it.'

'You've never lived with *anyone*?' she asked, a little astonished by the revelation—and the insight it gave her into his life.

She had known he was a lone wolf. It was all part of the Foxx brand. But had he always been alone, and why did that seem a little sad somehow? He'd mentioned the dysfunctional relationship he'd had with his father, but what about his mother? Or other carers and relatives? And why had he never lived with any of the many women he'd dated? She guessed commitment issues weren't uncommon in workaholic billionaires in their thirties. But what would that mean when he became a dad?

He shrugged again, but the movement was less relaxed. 'Not since I was a kid,' he said. 'And even then, I was always much better off on my own,' he clarified.

'Okay,' she said, feeling oddly bereft for him.

She'd always had Katie—even when her big sister was sofa surfing round London as a homeless teenager she'd kept in touch. And when Bea was really small, she'd had her Welsh grandmother too. She could still remember the cottage in Snowdonia where Angharad Evans had lived, and which Katie had eventually inherited. The warmth of the wood-burning stove on a rainy day, and the cosiness of the big brass bed upstairs where their *Nain* had told them bedtime stories about the mother who had loved them but had died too young.

Why would any child be better off without the security of being loved? Unless the people who were supposed to love them never had.

'Hey… It's not a big deal,' he said, taking the glass out of her hand and placing it on the breakfast bar. 'It's just easier if I don't live here.' Leaning against the marble bar, he took her hips in his hands and tugged her towards him. She braced her palms against his chest and felt his pectoral muscles flex and quiver—which sent sensation shooting into her panties. 'I don't want to keep you up at night waiting around for me… Unless I've got plans for you that don't involve sleeping.'

The suggestive gleam in his eyes had her choking out a laugh. And dispelled the moment of melancholy, which she was sure was his intention. But she let it go. She had time, lots of time, to find out more about his past and to quiz him about his plans for the future.

'Is everything always about sex with you?' she asked with mock outrage, as she threaded her fingers into his hair and tugged his lips closer.

'Pretty much,' he said, not sounding remotely apologetic as his devilish lips found the pulse point in her neck.

Before she could protest about his distraction techniques, or question him further, he boosted her into his arms.

'Come on, Princess,' he said, the old endearment making the throb in her abdomen rise to wrap around her heart.

'Practicalities later,' he declared. 'Naked fun now.'

As he marched down the hallway, she couldn't find the will to resist him.

Surely sex was a good way to increase the intimacy between them—and help them both relax and enjoy this new phase of their relationship, she reasoned.

And as his devious hands cupped her bottom, then sank into her panties, her anticipation peaked, and she concluded that sex certainly couldn't hurt.

Much, *much* later, she lay in a boneless heap, her body giddy with afterglow, on the bed where they had once made a baby, what felt like a lifetime ago, as he levered himself off the mattress.

She watched him dress, his muscular frame— and those fascinating scars and tattoos—gilded by the evening sunshine, while she resisted the pull of exhaustion and ignored the pang of dismay and regret.

Once he was fully clothed, he tucked her under the duvet, kissed her forehead and murmured, 'Later.'

But as the sound of his footsteps disappeared down the hallway and lulled her into a dreamless sleep, a thought drifted through her semiconsciousness…

They'd had lots of naked fun, but they hadn't sorted out any practicalities—except that his mouth was as versatile and inventive as the rest of him when it came to giving her multiple orgasms.

# CHAPTER TWELVE

*One month later*

'MASON, WE'VE GOT a table for you and Ms Medford for the Phoenix fundraiser tonight—just wanted to know if you're likely to attend,' asked John Taverner, Foxx's far too eager publicity manager. 'Joe told me to confirm directly with you.'

That was because his PA knew his social schedule was mostly blank now, Mason mused, taking in the view of Tower Bridge as the lift climbed to the top floor. Because he preferred to keep his evenings free—for booty calls with Beatrice.

He frowned. Booty calls, and too much more.

'We won't be there,' Mason murmured into his phone as the lift reached the penthouse. 'Give our apologies and add an extra hundred grand to the donation,' he finished, then cut off the call and shoved the phone into his pocket.

He'd escorted Beatrice to several events the first few weeks they'd been back in London. He'd enjoyed showing her off, plus he'd been convinced her presence on his arm—as the mother of his child—would enhance the Foxx brand. But he'd grown bored with that charade quickly, especially after he'd become aware how tired she got in the evenings.

At six months, her pregnancy was starting to take a toll on her energy levels, so it made sense not to parade her around tonight—and the press intrusion was always intense, so why encourage it?

He tore off his tie as the lift's doors opened. But as he dumped his briefcase on the hall table, unease skittered up his spine.

When exactly had he become such a home-body, more eager to spend time with her than promote his business?

He tried to shake off the uncomfortable thought, but as he stepped into the living area of the penthouse, his frown deepened and the muscles in his neck tightened.

He'd ensconced Beatrice here four weeks ago—specifically so he could keep his life separate from hers—but had spent pretty much every night since rushing back here to join her for dinner and sex after they both finished work.

He had always loved going to work, but the

struggle to leave Beatrice at dawn every morning—so he had time to return to his suite at Foxx Belgravia and prepare for the day—was real. And what the hell had happened to his work ethic these days?

He'd barely been able to concentrate on the string of meetings he'd had today about the new Foxx Motel chain they were building in the Hamptons, had even delegated the site visit to his New York executive team because he didn't want to spend time away from her. The whole project had begun to feel like a chore because his mind was always elsewhere. Such as this morning, when he had been fixated on the memory of Beatrice's breasts peeking over the duvet as she lay virtually comatose when he'd left.

Why couldn't he control the constant desire to be with her?

He'd started to look forward to their evenings together for a host of reasons and not just the sex. He loved hearing her eager observations about her new job—and was stupidly proud of what she had achieved in such a small space of time.

When he'd told his acquisitions team to find her a position which would utilise her language skills and had a competitive salary and benefits, he'd envisioned the job being busy work which would fulfil the promises he'd made to her in Portofino. But Beatrice had the work ethic of a Trojan and was a genuine polymath—according to her boss Jenna, who adored her—so she'd quickly made herself indispensable.

He appreciated her unique insights into his business initiatives too, in the conversations they shared about each other's day over take-away food, or their latest culinary disaster—because neither of them had any aptitude in the kitchen and he didn't want to hire staff when he wanted to be alone with her. He'd even started to enjoy her snippets of information about the pregnancy, perhaps because he had become unbearably curious about the life inside her too. Even though he shouldn't be.

He shrugged off his jacket and dumped it on the statement sofa—where he had brought her to a screaming orgasm last night after they'd watched one of the romcoms she loved. But he couldn't seem to shrug off the troubling direction of his thoughts.

How had he become so dependent on spending time with her? And why, when he found it so easy to deflect any probing questions about his past and their future, was he finding it a lot less easy to justify those deflections?

Perhaps because he'd become so aware of the

eager hope in Beatrice's eyes—every night he turned up back here again.

She wanted more than he could give her, he already knew that.

He should start preparing her for the time *after* the baby was born, when he wouldn't be around so much, if at all. Fatherhood was something he would suck at. So why couldn't he just tell her that?

'Beatrice?' he shouted, pushing the troubling thoughts to one side.

He still had three months to get round to that conversation. So what if he was enjoying spending time with her? He'd worked hard for years to get where he was today. And Beatrice had put in quite a shift herself since getting pregnant. The baby's arrival would put an end date on this interlude once and for all. So why shouldn't they enjoy it while they still could?

But when she didn't answer, his neck muscles tensed. Was she in the study again, working late?

He had come close to calling her boss Jenna today and demanding she ease up on Beatrice's workload, because he'd found her crouched over her computer yesterday evening. If Jenna had dumped a load more translations on her he wasn't going to hold off any longer—to hell with his decision not to interfere in her career...

But when he swung open the study door, he found the room empty.

He rubbed the back of his neck, in a vain attempt to massage away his frustration—and the tiny ripple of panic. So where was she then?

Hopefully not in the guest room, where she was setting up the nursery he had insisted on paying for but had been avoiding.

He headed down the hall towards the main bedroom.

But as he opened the door, he heard the shower running in the en suite bathroom. And the tension in his neck shot straight into his groin.

He walked silently into the bathroom, propelled by the familiar kick of arousal.

Perhaps all he'd really needed was to get laid. *Again*.

She stood in the glass cubicle with her body in profile, her face tilted into the stream. The treated glass gave him a clear view, despite the plume of steam rising from the hot jets. The flare of her hips and the curve of her breasts—which were getting heavier by the day—only added to the allure of her generous belly and her flushed skin, covered in soap.

A loud groan escaped as the kick of need sank deep.

Her head swung round. And their gazes locked.

Her face relaxed into a seductive smile—as she turned towards him, so he could look his fill. He drank in the sight like a man about to die of thirst. The water cascaded down her back and ran in rivulets over her full breasts. She cupped the heavy orbs, lifted and squeezed them, as if offering them to him, then grazed her thumbs over the engorged nipples.

He began shedding the rest of his clothing in a frantic rush. But as his cognitive abilities made a speedy exodus from his head, a new panic surfaced.

Why couldn't he stop wanting her? All the time. Seeing the changes his baby was making to her body was supposed to have weaned him off this addiction, but instead they only made him want her more.

But as he stripped off his shorts and walked to the cubicle, his mammoth erection leading the way—and watched her fingers trail down to her sex to torture him some more—he shoved the disturbing questions away.

Because he was way too desperate to touch her and taste her and torture her in return than to look for answers to any of them tonight.

The titanic orgasm cascaded through Bea with more force than the power shower pummelling them both. A guttural moan burst from her lips, her head dropping to rest against the shower tiles as she was catapulted onto the glittering cloud of afterglow.

Her hands slipped off Mason's shoulders, her back wedged against the quartz as he leaned against her. She buried her face into his neck, dragging in the scent of her vanilla soap on his skin, and loved the feel of his forearms flexing under her bare bottom as he held her aloft.

He shuddered violently through the last of his climax, while somehow managing to keep them both upright.

'Don't drop me,' she mumbled, her body massaging the thick length still impaling her.

He grunted in protest. 'Then stop that,' he remarked.

She let out a husky chuckle, still buoyed by the endorphin overload, reliving the memory of him stalking across the bathroom naked, his fierce expression promising retribution for her blatant provocation.

He groaned, then shifted against her, probably attempting a dismount. But as his flat stomach pressed against her belly, she felt the ripple of sensation deep in her abdomen which had started several weeks ago.

'What the hell was that?' He jerked back.

'You felt it too?' she asked, her heart bursting with joy.

'Yeah, what is it?'

She grinned, enjoying his stunned expression maybe a bit too much. She draped limp arms around his neck and wrapped her legs more securely around his waist, to anchor herself in his arms—after all, she was several pounds heavier than the first time they'd christened his shower.

'Answer me,' he said, impatience radiating off him. 'Are you okay?'

She nodded then smiled, pleased even more by his panicked reaction, because it was more concrete evidence of how much he worried about her welfare. Even if he wasn't ready to admit it. Yet.

'Absolutely,' she said, the joy in her heart all-consuming, because she was ridiculously happy they'd shared such an intimate moment. 'It's just the baby protesting at the squeeze on its living quarters.'

'That's…' He stared at the bump. 'Really?' Intense emotion flashed across his features but then his gaze became hooded, and he shifted away from her.

Her joy faded. A little.

The guarded expression was one she'd become accustomed to in the last four weeks. Every time she probed as gently as she could about his thoughts on the baby, or their future, or both.

His gaze glided down to where their bodies were still joined, but she could feel the tension in his shoulders increase—sense him distancing himself from the fierce excitement of moments ago.

'Good to know,' he said, his voice rough with all the things he refused to say.

More of the joy faded, replaced with sadness and confusion. Why did he find it so hard to talk about anything to do with the baby? He listened with interest when she gave him feedback about her antenatal appointments, but he never asked any questions. And he'd refused her invitation to attend her recent scan. And last week, when she'd asked if she could equip the guest bedroom as a nursery—hoping to start a conversation about what would happen once the baby was born—he gave her a gruff yes, then changed the subject by seducing her into a puddle of need on the dinner table.

The next day, his PA Joe had informed her of an account with unlimited funds set up in her name at London's most exclusive department store and supplied her with a list of personal shoppers who specialised in baby equipment and couture, and the contact details for a world-famous interior designer who did nursery interiors.

But Mason had refused to enter the guest room ever since.

Reaching across her, he switched off the still pounding jets. Then levered her off him to deposit her on her feet.

He clasped her elbow firmly, until he was sure she was steady.

'You good?' he asked.

'Yes,' she said, but as he let her go, she knew she wasn't good. Not even close.

Maybe the unshed tears making her eyes sting were the pregnancy hormones. Mostly. And the emotional wipeout of cataclysmic sex followed by feeling her baby move inside her and knowing he had felt it too. But all those qualifications couldn't dispel the ache when he left her standing alone in the shower to grab a towel.

She swallowed down the raw emotion pressing against her larynx as she watched him wrap it around his lean waist.

Why couldn't he let her know how he felt? Why couldn't he even talk about the baby? About them. About their future. She'd tried to be patient, tried to be understanding, tried to give him time to figure out his thoughts and feelings, because she suspected—from the little he'd let slip about his past—he wasn't a man used to having to talk about his emotional needs, or even really having to acknowledge he had any.

But she knew he did, because all the evidence

was already there—that he could be a tender, loving, fiercely protective father and partner, if he would just admit it to himself.

She'd seen the way he looked at her when he thought she wasn't watching. Had been able to read all the questions, all the need, in his eyes.

But it wasn't just the things he wouldn't say, it was the small ways in which he showed her she mattered.

He had hardly spent a single evening away from her since that first night when he had told her he needed separation. And he'd stopped leaving her to sleep alone. Now he always stayed the night and dragged himself away at stupid o'clock in the morning, so he would have time to return to his suite at the hotel in Belgravia where he kept all his clothing, but nothing else. He'd been agitated and tense when he found her working late yesterday but had stopped short of demanding she work less.

She'd become used to having him here most nights, used to the incredible sex, but also the feel of his strong arms around her when she slept, and the sight of him doing everything from attempting to cook a stir fry to snuggling up on the sofa so they could watch the romcoms she loved, which she knew he found boring. And she missed him on the very rare occasions when he didn't show.

She had become attached to him. Dependent on his company and his presence, and even on the in-depth discussions they'd had about her job and his work without ever getting a commitment out of him that he would still be here when she would need him most.

She shivered, stepping out of the cubicle. He lifted a towel off the pile and wrapped it around her shoulders.

'Listen, I need to go to an event tonight,' he said as he turned away to scoop his discarded clothing off the bathroom floor. 'I should probably head back to Belgravia to get changed,' he added.

She shuddered, the chill on her skin piercing her heart.

Was he really going to leave her straight after sex, for the first time in weeks? Spend the evening without her, when he had never done that, not once since she'd been back in London? Right after feeling the baby move for the first time.

'Do you want me to come with you?' she asked hopefully, sure she must have misunderstood.

They'd been to several events when she'd first arrived, and she'd enjoyed being seen with him, but the press attention had been insane, and she'd nearly fallen asleep at a banquet in the Barbican—so she had also been stupidly pleased when he'd stopped suggesting they attend public engagements. But she wanted to go with him now, somehow scared by what this might mean.

He glanced at her, but his gaze darted away again before she could gauge his reaction.

'No need,' he said. 'It's likely to be a late one. And you must be tired. I'll probably crash at the hotel tonight.'

The oh-so-casual dismissal felt like a physical blow, his desire to leave, to pull away from her, suddenly making her question all the assumptions she'd made about how he really felt. About her, about the baby, about them.

Good God, had she been kidding herself all along? Wanting to believe he felt more for her than he did? Wasn't that exactly what she'd done with her father for years? Believed he loved her and cared for her, and that if she just did as he wanted, he would eventually show her she had value to him, instead of just being a means to an end?

'How important is this event?' she asked as her heart buffeted her chest, making the stinging pain in her eyes intensify.

He stared at her blankly.

'It's just, you didn't mention it until now,' she added. 'And I wondered why.'

But when he continued to stare at her, she knew why. This was just another of his avoidance tactics. Another chance for him not to acknowledge his feelings.

She had seen that moment of awe in his eyes when he'd felt the baby move too, before it had disappeared. But she clung to it now.

Time was galloping away from them. Soon they would have a child, and she still had no idea if he wanted to be a permanent part of its life. Or even how he really felt about her. Because she had failed to ask.

And failed to hold him to account.

There were so many other things she didn't know about him because she had sensed his reluctance to talk about them. And being sensitive to his needs had been easier than facing her oldest fear, that if she asked for more, she would be told she wasn't worthy, she wasn't enough.

Yet none of that had stopped her falling in love with him… The thought blindsided her.

*Wow, Bea, fabulous time to figure that out.*

But it also galvanised her. Because loving him wasn't enough. She had to know if there was a chance that he could love her in return. Or else she would be trapped in another one-sided relationship—where she was left hoping for the unconditional love she needed, instead of demanding it.

Apparently, her old fear of confrontation had reared its ugly head again over the past month. The same cowardice which had allowed her to live in her father's house for so long and never challenge his agenda. She'd never pushed Mason about when he was coming over, she'd simply been overjoyed to see him. She'd never asked for a commitment other than what he was willing to give…

How had she allowed herself to slip into that passive role with Mason when there was so much at stake?

Perhaps because she had convinced herself she was different now. But having a fulfilling job, and great sex, and knowing he cared about her—in a way her father never had—wasn't enough. Not for her or her baby.

'Yeah, it's pretty important,' he said. 'I should go.' But she could hear the lie in his voice because she had become much better at reading him now.

A single tear escaped, but she scrubbed it away.

'Beatrice? What's wrong?' he said, sounding pained. And so, so wary. 'It's just one night, okay?'

'Except it's not just about tonight, Mason,' she said, suddenly feeling unbearably weary and unsure of herself.

'What's that supposed to mean?' he demanded.

'You never want to talk to me…'

'I talk to you all the time,' he interrupted her, but she recognised the tactic, although it wasn't one he'd used before—belligerence and indignation to avoid the truth. 'I'm here pretty much every night, *all* night, and I've let my other commitments slide. But I can't keep doing that.'

'You never want to talk to me about the baby, about us,' she said slowly, carefully, determined to pierce the bubble of outrage, knowing she couldn't let him derail her or distract her again.

She had to find her courage now. The courage she'd taken for granted, but which she needed more than ever.

'About how you feel about fatherhood,' she continued. She cupped her stomach, the little flutter there reassuring her and bolstering her determination. 'And what you envisage your role being in this baby's life. In *my* life, after it's born.'

'Why do we need to talk about that right now? We've got months yet before it's even born,' he snapped, but she could hear the fear now too.

'Because I want you to be a part of my life,' she said. 'So much.' She took a deep breath.

She had to tell him the truth too, however exposed it made her feel. Which was a lot.

'Because I've fallen in love with you, Mason. And I want us to be a family.'

# CHAPTER THIRTEEN

'YOU DON'T LOVE ME, PRINCESS,' Mason said, trying for flippant, even as everything inside him felt raw and exposed. Feeling those little kicks inside her had shocked him and excited him, but then they had crucified him.

He should have seen this coming, should have realised that someone like Beatrice would make the mistake of thinking he was a good guy. Because he'd been too scared to tell her the truth.

'Don't tell me how I feel,' she said.

'Then don't say stupid things. How can you love me when you don't even know me?' Mason replied as the panic clawed at his throat.

She'd never looked more beautiful than in that moment, he realised, standing in nothing but a towel, her damp curls flattened against her head, her gaze open and generous and direct. And full of an innocence he had always lacked.

But she'd also never looked more vulnerable, her stunning bone structure so fragile, her eyes—those huge blue orbs—so innocent. And so full of hope.

He hadn't wanted to tell her about himself, about his past, about all the things he'd done to survive. The stuff he'd covered up and ignored and never had a problem with until she'd come into his life.

But as he watched her cradle the mound of her belly where their baby grew, he figured he was all out of options now.

Did she even know she was doing that? Instinctively protecting their child from the likes of him.

She blinked slowly, her eyes blank with shock, but then they filled with the shimmer of compassion which only made the guilty hole in his gut swell. And twist.

'What don't I know about you, Mason?' she said with a confidence he knew she'd worked so hard to earn. 'If it's so terrible, don't you think it's about time you told me?'

He would have done anything not to burst the bubble, not to destroy her hope. Because in his own way he knew he had deep feelings for her too. And the baby. Feelings he'd tried hard not to admit. To himself as well as her. To protect them both.

'You really want to know?' he said. 'I'll tell

you, but I suggest we both get dressed first,' he finished, before stalking out of the bathroom.

He took his time getting his clothes back on, his whole body shaking, pathetically grateful when she didn't follow him out immediately. He couldn't do this while they were both naked because it already felt like trying to tear off his own skin.

He was slipping on his shoes when she appeared, wearing a bathrobe, her hair brushed, her face still flushed from her shower and their lovemaking. The thought of never being able to touch her again, to hold her, to make her shudder and moan, to watch her going over with that stunned pleasure on her face felt unbearable. But somehow much worse was the thought of never having her look at him again with that tenderness in her eyes.

He'd always considered himself a selfish man, only interested in dating for the physical pleasure he could get out of it. So why did that thought hurt most of all?

He sat down on the bed. Rested his forearms on his knees. Suddenly exhausted, as all the convenient lies, the easy deflections, the endless avoidance tactics had finally deserted him.

She opened her mouth to say something, but he beat her to it.

'Why do you love me?' The question burst out before he could think it through.

He cringed. How needy and pathetic was that?

He'd expected contempt, maybe even derision, but when her gaze searched his, all he saw was compassion. And that crippling tenderness that made him feel like that little boy again, wanting and waiting for something that he could never have.

'Oh, Mason,' she said. 'Why would I not fall in love with you?' She tucked her hand over her bump. 'You gave me a baby, and in many ways you also gave me my freedom.' She sighed. 'It hurt to hear it at the time, but you were right about what I'd allowed myself to become because I was too scared to stand up to my father.'

'That's nonsense, Beatrice,' he said. 'You would have figured it out eventually, without me seducing you and getting you pregnant, then dumping you the very next day in the most callous way imaginable.'

He'd apologised for the way he'd spoken to her that morning. But the more he'd thought about the way he'd behaved in the last month, the more he'd realised an apology wasn't enough.

She cleared her throat, the pale blue of her eyes sparkling. 'Excuse me, but who seduced whom that first night? Because I'm pretty sure you've got that the wrong way round.'

He let out a brittle laugh. God, she was adorable. But the ripple of amusement faded almost as quickly as it had come.

He looked away from her because he couldn't look at her and explain the rest.

'You want to know why you really had to leave Italy?' he managed.

'Why…' she asked, so sweet, so trusting.

He blew out a breath and pushed the words out. 'I told Joe to tip off the press.'

The murmured confession felt like a gunshot. Her eyebrows lifted but the tenderness remained, because she didn't seem to be able to process the whole sordid truth.

'I forced your hand,' he explained. 'Because I didn't want to wait. And I convinced myself that what I wanted was the only thing that mattered,' he raced on, the hideous reality of what he'd done starting to strangle him. 'So instead of allowing you to make your own decision, I went behind your back to stack the odds in my favour.'

He could still remember her stubborn determination not to give in to his demands in the pizzeria in Rapallo. Her insistence that she needed to be independent. And, in a lot of ways, he'd admired her for it. But when the press hordes had descended the next morning, it hadn't taken him long to qualify his actions and justify doing whatever was necessary to get what he wanted.

It was what he'd always done. Deflect, evade and cover up the truth until things went the way he wanted them to. That was the real man behind the myth. Not the self-made billionaire who had worked his way up from nothing, taken insane risks and reaped the hoped-for rewards, but the boy who even a mother couldn't love. The boy who had done terrible things to escape his fate.

And he could see so clearly now. He hadn't forced her hand to protect her or the baby, which was what he'd told himself at the time, but because he'd been terrified, even then, that, given the choice, she wouldn't choose him.

He heard her let out a breath and he braced himself for her anger, and her disgust.

But when she eventually spoke, all he heard in her voice was that same compassion.

'Well, I'm glad you told me about that, and it was a pretty sneaky thing to do,' she said, in what had to be the understatement of the century. But then her delicate hand landed on his knee, and she squeezed it softly. 'But FYI, I think you only really speeded up the inevitable.'

He turned to her, shocked by the easy affection in her tone—and the quiet acceptance.

'*Really?* Beatrice? That's it?' he said, starting to feel annoyed now. 'That's all you've got to say? I manipulated you. I ripped you away from a life you loved and had spent months building for yourself and I took away all your choices—and you're just gonna forgive me for it?' Make that a lot annoyed.

'Well, to be fair, I really didn't love scrubbing toilets *that* much,' she said.

'This isn't a joke.' He dragged a hand through his hair, then stood and paced to the window, unable to sit still. And unable to have her look at him like that, as if what he'd done didn't matter, when he knew it did.

He swore softly. 'Is this some leftover from that bastard who fathered you? That you think you have to accept my bad behaviour because you love me,' he said, doing sarcastic air quotes, because he was just that mad.

'No, it's not.'

She jumped up and crossed the room, the quiet acceptance gone. *Finally.*

'And if you ever do something like that again…' Her chest puffed up and her gaze narrowed. 'You will definitely be sorry.'

Which would have been more of a threat if he wasn't so sorry already.

'But it seems to me you've tortured yourself enough so there's not much point in me torturing you too. And the fact you told me what you did is important. Because now we can have trust.'

'Trust?' he murmured. Did she even know what that meant? How could she be so gullible…? He cupped her neck, pressed his forehead to hers, unable not to touch her this one last time. 'How can you trust me, Beatrice, if you don't know who I really am?'

The panic blocked his throat again as she cradled his cheek.

'I think you'd better tell me the rest of it, Mason,' she said softly.

He nodded, knowing she was right. It hurt like hell to know that once he told her all the things he'd done she wouldn't love him any more. But what would hurt more was continuing to manipulate her, continuing to play on her innocence and tenderness for his own ends.

He lifted his head, walked back to the window and looked down at the docks where he'd once worked for villains and dreamed about getting away. Getting out.

Funny to think he'd always remained trapped there without even realising it. The instincts he'd always been so proud of, for self-preservation and self-denial, born of being that boy who would do anything to escape.

'I told you my old man was a bastard,' he said slowly, carefully. 'That he used me. But the truth is, he was just a stupid loser with an addiction he couldn't control. He'd bet on anything—the greyhounds, the horses, on whether West Ham would score in the second minute or the tenth. And because of that, we were always dead broke.'

That life seemed so far away now—being scared in the winter to turn on the heating, eating cereal for tea because there was nothing else in the house, and being the smelly kid in school because you didn't have the pennies for the laundrette. But, in so many ways, that life had always remained inside him. Because he'd never really shaken off the fear of being a failure like his old man.

And wasn't that why he'd worked so hard to get out? Not to be rich, but to be safe.

Her footsteps padded across the carpet, then her cheek rested on his back. He shuddered, the soft touch both reassuring and terrifying. Because he wanted it so much, he needed it, and he wasn't sure he could survive losing it.

'Mason, it's okay. Breathe,' she murmured, but his legs had turned to jelly, the emotion like a tidal wave, threatening to knock him off his feet.

He braced his legs to stay upright as the memories swirled, no longer tethered in the deep recesses of his mind but choking him with guilt and remorse.

The memory of sitting on the wall outside the basement hovel where he had once lived, each day after school, for weeks and weeks, waiting for his mum to come back, shimmered on the edges of his consciousness, damning him even more. But worse was the memory of his old man's face—tired, worn, terrified—years later, the last time he'd seen him.

'Eventually, he owed money to loan sharks. A *lot* of money. And the only way we could pay off the debts was for me to run errands for them.' He forced himself to draw in another painful breath and let it out, her presence at his back the only thing anchoring him to the here and now. 'I did it for a while. I even enjoyed it at first, because they'd give me tips.' He shrugged. 'But then, eventually, I didn't want to do it any more. I was older, smarter. I saw what they did—the people they beat up for nothing, the women they exploited. I was scared of them, and terrified I'd get caught eventually and be stuck in that life for ever. So I told my dad I was leaving.' He stared down at his feet, the polished leather of his designer brogues reflecting his own face back at him. But all he could see in that moment was his old man begging. 'And I never looked back.'

Bea reached around his waist to hold him, her heart shattering as she tried to soothe the shivers she could feel racing through him. She heard the shame in his voice.

'And you blame yourself for that?' she asked softly.

Was this the root? The reason why he had been so determined to hold a part of himself back? Because he had been scared to trust her with his demons?

She'd assumed this was all about her. That she hadn't been strong enough, smart enough, brave enough to demand what she needed from him. That because she'd fallen in love with him, she had been too scared to press the point in case he rejected her.

And there was some truth in that…

But, deep down, she could see now that this wasn't just about her confidence, it was also about his. They had both been broken by things outside their control and plunged into an emotional storm neither of them had had the tools to negotiate without making mistakes.

'Yeah, I do,' he said, his voice breaking. 'They were pretty specific. They told me if I didn't do what they said they'd kill him. So I did what they said. Even though I knew it was wrong.'

He heaved out a breath, his shoulders shaking, his voice a monotone as he continued.

'But when I was fourteen, I'd had enough. I didn't care what happened to him any more.' He turned, the look in his eyes so bleak, she shuddered. 'He begged me not to go, and I left anyway. And I never saw him again after that. I doubt what they did to him was pretty,' he finished. 'How can you love *that* man? A man who would do that to his own flesh and blood to save himself. Why would you want to have a person like that around your baby?'

'Because he wasn't a man, he was a child, Mason,' she said softly, wanting him to see what she saw when she looked at him.

But he simply shook his head. 'I was old enough.'

She saw the hopelessness in his expression and realised she was seeing a window into his past, a glimpse of the boy inside the man. And the impossible challenges he'd faced. The struggles he'd overcome. The terrible price he'd paid for that. Alone and resentful and desperate to find a way out—just as she had been when she'd first met him.

He'd given her a way out, however inadvertently—by challenging her to see who she had allowed herself to become.

She'd discovered in Italy that she could grow and change—by standing up for herself. But she'd never stopped blaming herself for her past cowardice, or she wouldn't have fallen in love with him without accepting he had some terrible insecurities too.

'So now you know,' he said, dropping his head. He rubbed his thumb over the bird in flight etched on the back of his hand. 'I'm a fraud. I built an empire on the back of that betrayal.' His head lifted, the naked honesty in his eyes raw with vulnerability. 'In my defence, the things I did, and the lies I told you to get you to want me, to get you to stay, are nothing compared to the lies I've told myself over the years.'

Her heart broke at the self-loathing in his voice. But, after the pieces had shattered in her chest, she felt the sure, steady beat of her love—and knew it was strong enough and wise enough to see his flaws, as well as her own, and to accept them.

She cupped his cheek, the joy in her chest immense when he leaned into the caress instinctively.

'I guess neither of us is perfect then,' she said softly, her lips quirking. 'How annoying.'

His brows lifted, the stunned disbelief in his

eyes almost as painful as the ache in her chest where her heart was pounding so hard she was surprised it didn't burst.

He covered her hand with his, drew it away from his face then threaded his fingers through hers and held on. 'You don't want to leave me?'

Her lips lifted and she shook her head as it occurred to her that this was the easiest answer she'd ever had to give anyone.

'I told you I love you. Now do you believe me?' she asked.

His green eyes turned a rich emerald, the wicked sparkle making her heart hurt. 'If you say so, Princess.'

Lifting her fingers to his mouth, he pressed an earnest, reverent kiss to her knuckles. The familiar awareness sank into her abdomen.

'If it's any consolation,' he added, 'I think I love you too.' He glanced down at her stomach. 'And the bump.'

Her eyebrow lifted. 'You think, or you know?'

He wrapped his arms around her waist and lifted her. She clasped his shoulders, looking down into his harsh, handsome face as the rich emerald softened with love.

'I know,' he said.

She grinned down at him. Their baby's movements fluttered in her belly, as if it was adding its approval. 'You'd better not forget that when the bump is waking you up at two in the morning, wanting to be fed.'

He laughed, a deep, throaty, relieved laugh which made the joy spread and glow in her chest. 'You do know you're the one with the equipment to sort that out, right?' he offered, the arrogance she had come to adore returning.

He lowered her slowly, then reached inside her robe to caress said equipment possessively—and reiterate his point.

She clasped his wrist, the giddy need firing down to her toes. But she looked him straight in the eye when she said, 'I guess that leaves you on nappy duty then.'

They were both still chuckling as they fell onto the bed to concentrate on tearing each other's clothes off.

# EPILOGUE

*One year later*

'UP YOU GO, Princess Trouble!' Mason grinned.
The Riviera sunshine sparkled on the water of
the *castello*'s new infinity pool as he boosted
his tiny daughter into the air.

Her belly laughs as he caught her again had
him beaming back at her. Then his own laughter burst free when she kicked her arms and legs
furiously—which was her not so subtle way of
demanding Daddy do it again, *immediately*.

At eight months old, Ella Carys Angharad
Foxx was an absolute tyrant who had her father
wrapped firmly around her plump little finger.
Her mother had warned him he was creating a
monster. But he adored hearing his daughter's
laughter and he hated hearing her cry—so he
was usually very amenable to her requests.

But when she rubbed her eyes, while trying
to launch herself out of his arms again, he re-

alised this was one of those times he was going to have to disappoint her.

'That's all, Cinders,' he said, touching a finger to her adorable button nose, which was starting to look slightly pink. 'We don't want you getting a sunburn or Daddy will be in the doghouse tonight.'

And he had plans for this evening which did not involve soothing an unhappy baby, because it would be the anniversary of the day he'd told her mother the truth about his past, and she'd decided to love him anyway.

The smile sank into his heart as he tucked his daughter under his arm to wade out of the water. She carried on wriggling and chortling, because she thought this was a brand-new game. There would be tired tears in his near future when she figured out this new game was called naptime.

He walked over to the pool loungers, where Jack Wolfe was reading a book of fairy tales to his oldest son, Luca.

The four-year-old pointed at one of the illustrations. 'Mummy says that's you, Daddy,' the little boy announced.

'Your mother said I was the big, bad wolf? What the...?' Jack frowned, managing to cut off the swearword, while sending Mason a wry look.

'Own it, bro,' Mason replied, laughing as he

grabbed a towel and began stripping off Ella's sunsuit.

He and Jack had become fast friends, ever since the guy had offered to walk Beatrice down the aisle at their wedding that spring—because her father had resolutely refused to do it unless Mason paid him five grand for the privilege. He had considered paying the money because he knew Beatrice still struggled with her father's refusal to speak to her, but Jack had advised him not to.

*'He doesn't deserve either one of his daughters. I'm guessing, in her heart, Bea knows that, because she's not stupid. And, believe me, you and your family do not need someone that toxic in your life, at any price.'*

He'd had to agree with the guy.

He hadn't told Beatrice about her father's demand. She did not need to know the man was still a Class A ass, determined to remain estranged from both his daughters. But he'd been relieved when she had seemed more than happy to have her brother-in-law as a substitute.

The fact that Beatrice and Jack had once been engaged might have made Wolfe 'giving her away' super weird. The glossy magazines had certainly gone into gossip overload when unauthorised photos of the wedding had hit the internet. But Mason hadn't cared how it looked.

Because when Beatrice had appeared at the end of the aisle on Jack's arm, dressed in a silk wedding gown which shimmered in the candlelight and made his breath back up in his lungs, he knew his bride had only ever had eyes for him.

And the Wolfes were family now.

Jack and Katherine's three sons—because her second pregnancy had turned out to be twins, to everyone's shock, especially Katherine's—would be playmates for Ella, and all the other kids he was hoping to make with her mummy one day. So they had been more than happy to invite the Wolfes to join them this summer in Portofino, once he'd finished having the old Grande Hotel where Beatrice had once worked converted into a luxury fifteen-room *castello*, for their exclusive use.

Beatrice hadn't been super-keen on the idea when he'd first bought the place as a wedding present for her. Until he'd got her to admit the reason why... She was concerned that her friends at the Portofino Grande would lose their jobs.

So he'd decided to buy a string of resorts in the region to launch Foxx Italia in Liguria and appointed Marta and Fabrizio to head the executive team to oversee the renovations and relocation of the staff. A win-win—not only as a sound business investment but also as a way to show Beatrice that he respected her input and they would always be a team.

'Wave goodbye to Uncle Jack and cousin Luca,' he said, propping the freshly changed Ella onto his shoulder. She was getting fussy. Probably because, being smart as a whip, she had figured out the new game wasn't nearly as much fun as the old one.

'See you later, Ella,' said Jack.

Luca waved enthusiastically, before continuing the in-depth discussion he'd been having with his father. 'The Big Bad Wolf is not a mis-pun-derstood wolf, Daddy,' he said, mispronouncing the word with considerable gravity. 'He's a very naughty wolf.'

Mason was still laughing as he headed into the house.

His daughter got crankier while he had a conversation with the head chef, who wanted to brief him on tonight's dinner menu, and a chat with his sister-in-law, who was looking suitably pleased with herself after having got twins Cai and Dafydd down for their nap with the help of the nanny they'd hired for the summer.

By the time he and Ella arrived in the Presidential Suite, his daughter was making her feelings known in no uncertain terms. And they were not happy ones.

He felt bad about her tears as he tried to

soothe her, but it was hard for him to feel anything but a swift kick of joy when her mother rushed out of the bathroom.

Although the suite of rooms looked totally different from last summer, with all the new fixtures and fittings bringing it bang up-to-date, he recognised the fierce emotion that flowed through him as he spotted her. Because he'd felt something similar when he'd first seen Beatrice walk out of that bathroom with a bucket and mop, her hair shorter than it was now, and her figure round with the baby he now held in his arms.

He hadn't understood it then, but he did now as his wife rushed up to them both and scooped the loudly protesting Ella out of his arms.

'Uh-oh, has Princess Trouble got overtired?' she said, sending him an amused and slightly smug smile over the tuft of blonde hair on their daughter's head—which made her look like a cute, and currently very indignant, dandelion.

'Yeah, a little too much fun in the sun with Daddy again,' he murmured ruefully as Beatrice settled herself and the crying baby on the bedroom's generous sofa and released her breast from the nursing bra.

The emotion he hadn't figured out then was easy to figure out now, he thought as he sat beside them and slung his arm around his wife's shoulders, while his daughter latched onto her plump nipple as if she hadn't been fed in a month.

Shock and awe, fierce pride and total, all-consuming love.

'Success!' Bea whispered triumphantly as she eased the door closed to her daughter's bedroom.

Was there anything more wonderful than watching your child falling into a deep, peaceful sleep?

'That's only because you have all the right equipment,' Mason quipped as his strong arms wrapped around her from behind and he tugged her back against his chest. 'You cheated.'

She turned in his arms and laughed, delighted with them both. And the incredible life they'd made for each other. As well as the fact that their daughter would now be asleep for several precious hours when his hands strayed down to her bottom and squeezed.

'You're just jealous,' she teased. 'Because I am the Queen of the Magic Boobies.'

He chuckled. 'Not true, Queen,' he said, boosting her into his arms and walking her backwards towards their bedroom, the provocative look in his eyes full of the hot promise she adored. 'Because I happen to love your magic boobies too.'

She was still laughing as he dumped her onto the bed, but it wasn't long before he had turned her triumph into a quivering mass of desperate need.

Half an hour later, Bea lay, limp and well-satisfied, in his arms, watching the early evening light turn a rich blue on the horizon.

'So then Luca says, "He's not a misunderstood wolf, he's a naughty wolf". You should have seen the expression on Jack's face, it cracked me up,' Mason said as his fingers stroked her arm lazily.

She chuckled, delighted not just at the conversation between Jack and his son, which did sound hilarious, but also that her sister's family and theirs had become so close. She loved that Jack and Mason had become good friends. She suspected that Mason didn't have many men he could really confide in, because all his friends seemed to work for him. She also knew, from what Katie had told her about Jack's childhood, that the two men had much more in common than Mason realised.

'Katie's hilarious,' she said. 'She told me her and Jack's relationship is *Little Red Riding Hood*, but I wouldn't laugh too hard because she's decided our relationship is a specific fairy tale too.'

'Oh, yeah, which one?' Mason asked. *'The Giant that got the Golden Goose?'* he teased.

She huffed, then flipped over and propped her elbows onto his chest to give him a mock stern look. 'Are you calling me a goose, Mr Foxx?'

His gaze drifted up to her hair, which she suspected was a total mess, but all she saw was rich appreciation in his eyes when his gaze dropped down to hers again. 'I'm calling you golden, Mrs Foxx.'

'Nice save,' she said, and kissed him. Before they could get carried away again, though, she pulled back. 'Apparently, our fairy tale is *Rapunzel.* Because you saved me from my ivory tower.' She brushed her hand over her unruly curls, which she now kept in a manageable bob. 'And I lost my long golden locks in the process.'

He choked out a laugh but then skewered her again with that appreciative look that always made her feel cherished and seen. 'Hey, you know what? I like it,' he announced. 'I think it totally fits.'

'You do?' she said, astonished that he had bought into Katie's whimsical metaphor because, as much as she adored this man, he was far too real and rugged and rough around the edges to be the fairy tale type.

He rolled on top of her. 'Totally,' he said.

The tension at her core clenched and released

deliciously as his newly perked up erection brushed against her belly and she calculated if they had enough time for another round before Ella woke up.

She certainly hoped so.

He hooked her hair behind her ear. 'Because that makes me a handsome prince, right?' he added, the smug smile clear in his tone as he nuzzled the sensitive spot on her neck he knew would drive her wild. 'Instead of the Big, Bad Wolf.'

\* \* \* \* \*

*If the drama of*
Hidden Heir with His Housekeeper
*blew you away, then why not explore these other stories by Heidi Rice?*

*Available now!*